Deception Pass

by

Norm Harris

Deception Pass

Cover Art by *Diana Carlile*

The Wild Rose Press, Inc.
PO Box 708
Adams Basin, NY 14410-0708
Visit us at www.thewildrosepress.com

Publishing History
First Edition, 2022
Trade Paperback ISBN 978-1-5092-4187-3
Digital ISBN 978-1-5092-4188-0

Published in the United States of America

Fay sensed the presence of Death around her. In the curtains, in the book placed on the nightstand next to the bed. Even in the sunlight streaming through the window across the bed. Death lurked everywhere.

Although she had experienced Death before, including three of her own near-death experiences, Navy Judge Advocate Commander Faydra Green had not gotten used to his genius. Then again, Death was not a person. Although he was, without a doubt, a man. His costume was complete with a giant sling blade and a black hooded cape shrouding his white, pasty face.

Those closest to her seemed to die. Her mother had died twenty-eight years before in an automobile accident. An accident had left her half-sister, JP Fletcher, injured and near death. Her father, former United States President William Green, had died a little over two years ago. And she had killed a man. Oh yes, Fay knew Death quite well.

Praise for Norm Harris

"…a smart, believable suspense filled mystery. Military enthusiasts will find Norm Harris's penchant for accuracy refreshing."

~ Cal Glomstad, former CBS News-reporter, CTE/Contemporary World Issues/Instructor, WYA-Washington State Military Department.

"Norm Harris's book grabs the reader with its first sentence and holds the reader throughout with its fast-paced action. Dialogue is always the hard-est to write, but Harris has captured the art and with his writing keeps the reader turning pages, his ability to heighten the intrigue keeps the reader on the edge of his or her seat throughout the story. Strongly recommend the book."

~ CAPT David E. Meadows, US Navy, author of numerous military thrillers such as Sixth Fleet, Seawolf, and Tomcat.

Dedication

For my son, Kristopher-Kent Herbert Harris, with love and amazement.

IN MEMORY
Josephine Hindman, Gladys Richardson, Nell Gelis, Eunice Harris, and Jack Brix.

Acknowledgments

Many thanks to those friends and associates who made this book happen, be it for your technical advice, editing, proofreading, or simply moral support: Jeanette Lundgren Navy Captain David Meadows, Carolyn Starr, Alexis Singleton "Attorney at Law", and Sheriff Jack Gardner. A special thank you goes out to Kathleen Jackson, and Mom and Dad. Thank you all for both your inspiration and valued friendships.

A special thank you to Carolyn Shafer for her superb edit and proofreading.

Prologue

A tall woman with auburn hair sat on a stool next to a man in the Mercure Arbat Moscow Lobby Bar. She did not acknowledge him. After dropping her purse on the floor, she ordered champagne. When the drink arrived, she downed it in one swallow.

She pulled a black 9mm GSh-18 pistol from her purse, pointed it at the man, and fired. The man recoiled backward from the stool, landing at her feet on the floor. The noisy lounge became silent in an instant. All eyes were on the woman, who stood, without looking at the man, dropped the black 9mm into her purse and walked through the club's entrance, vanishing into the stream of afternoon strollers on the Arbat.

Chapter 1

Prison 2, Beijing, China, three months earlier
On an evening in February, one of the prisoners, H344257, was sitting on his bunk, as he did every evening, his bare feet planted firmly on the warm concrete floor. From his small cell window, he could just see the top of the Beijing city skyline. He watched through the window, his custom every evening, as a prison vehicle arrived in the courtyard below. The prisoner transfer vehicles all looked like hearses and, well, they should.

It was the same procedure each evening. New prisoners arrived, and a smaller number departed. His accounting was accurate to the man. He thought it a pity how the guards seemed to take great pride in their intimidation of the new prisoners, yet they seemed to fear the older ones. Or perhaps, they were showing their respect?

There were always three guards riding in the prison vehicle: one, a driver, and two others. Tonight, he counted twice the number. He wondered about it; there were always three. Perhaps one or more of the new arrivals needed extra security? The prisoner vehicle always arrived at the same time; it always departed at the same time.

When the show was over, he would rise from his bunk and make his way to the metal toilet below his window. He was proud of his toilet, one of the few with a lid. Although, it had been a while since his toilet had been cleaned or disinfected. He had long stopped worrying about bacteria. It seemed the toilet had not been cleaned before his occupation of this cell.

After three months in Prison 2, he had gotten used to his stinking cell hell. No one bothered him; perhaps Americans received preferential treatment? The guards appeared to be astonished; on each visit to his cell, they covered their noses.

He was allowed to go outside for 120 minutes each day to walk the prison grounds alone; he could not contact any of the other prisoners. He could not speak Chinese anyway. His guard decided when he would and should go outside, and his guard determined how much time he would spend outdoors. It would take only a tiny amount of coin to buy him more time outdoors, but he was saving his money for a blanket. Five years ago, he had been one of the wealthiest men in America. Today, he was the poorest schmuck in China.

His downfall had begun with the bitch lawyer. Chicago crime boss Joey "The Guppy" Stumpanato had hired her for no other reason than to cause him grief. The goddamn whore had set him up - big time. He had been a mob lawyer once, just like her. He should have seen it coming. He should have killed her when he had had the chance. He had tried - twice! She had managed to foil his attempts. And she had dared to try to kill him! Imagine it!

"Goddamn bitch," he muttered. "Some day, some way," he swore.

Cell blocks in Prison 2 were known by their telephone number. His was 42-14435. Why not reach out and touch someone? Although he had become accustomed to his cell's repugnant air, his occasional bouts of insomnia kept him awake at night. Did he hear what sounded like a helicopter?

The crazy portion of the prison population remained vocal late into the night. Be it the screams of a tortured or tormented soul or the singing of the woman prisoners, noise always prevailed. Yet, he managed to hang on to his sanity.

The guards played a cute trick; fortunately, they had not yet played it on him. Prisoners were placed in wooden boxes, not much larger than a coffin. They were awakened at dawn, blindfolded, and made to sit upright in the box, facing straight ahead until evening. They were not allowed to talk; the penalty for any infringement of the rule was the whip.

This could go on for days until the prisoner broke. Some of them went mad. Or so he had been told. He now realized this night that the incessant noise had ceased. In an instant, an explosion rocked him from his bunk and collapsed his cell door.

Men were yelling as they burst into his cell. His arms were tied behind his back; they placed a bag over his head.

"Move it!" a male voice demanded in English. The figure sounded like an American.

The perplexed prisoner was escorted – more like pushed - into what he thought to be the prison transport van - the same van he had observed delivering prisoners earlier in the day. He could only hear. Yet, no one spoke.

The prisoner rode in the swelting van for maybe thirty minutes. The van came to a halt.

The voice ordered, "Move it." He could hear what

he presumed to be men scrambling. Everyone seemed to be in a hurry.

Next, he heard the thumping of what he knew to be a helicopter as its engines began to wind up. Things looked hopeful. Who were these people managing his escape? And why?

Once aboard, he sensed the chopper lift from the ground, roll forward, and continue on its flight path. Someone fastened a seatbelt around him to secure him from falling out.

He thought he recognized a voice. His photographic memory would not play tricks on him. They had left him bound but not gagged. They must not trust him. In the meantime, he continued to focus on the voice of the man. When the stranger spoke, there was no doubt about it. He recognized the voice.

"Where am I? Who are you?" he asked.

No response. Someone placed a set of headphones on his head. And while he could no longer hear his captors conversing, he could hear the chopper pilots when they spoke to anyone. He found it fascinating.

He learned they were traveling across the land, flying at a cruising altitude of 10,000 feet; he knew it was the optimal maneuvering atmosphere. Higher than 10K, the air grew thinner, causing the blades to work harder to generate the same lift. The pilots received and gave directions and other status reports to someone who spoke English and Russian. *What a great mystery*, he thought to himself. He continued to listen.

One of his captors slipped a straw under his hood. "*Zhadno vpityvat*, comrade," the voice said in Russian. *("Drink in, friend")*.

"*Spacibo,*" the prisoner replied. Although warm, it

proved to be the best water he had enjoyed in a very long time.

He estimated they had been traveling for about one hour. He was unsure of their direction, until he began to smell seawater. This meant they had traveled east from Beijing and toward the ocean. If so, they were heading toward the Yellow Sea. And beyond?

The chopper seemed large. Assuming it flew at a ground speed of about one hundred sixty miles per hour and allowing for a three hundred service range, this would place them over the Yellow Sea. He estimated they were three hundred thirty miles east of the Chinese coastline. A one-way trip. If their destination were indeed a ship, this meant the ship would be large enough to include a helipad.

Occasionally, he could hear the conversation between the pilots and their target. The languages were mixed, but he did understand minimal Russian and was getting better at it.

Codenames were used, to some extent. They were "Kobold Two," and they communicated with someone referred to as "Kitty Hawk." He supposed it to be a ship. Or perhaps an island? The jury was still out which flag their target flew: Old Glory or *Rossiskoy Federatsi*. If he remained patient, he would soon know.

Although he could not distinguish what those around him were saying, he could tell by their hurried activity a change had occurred. He waited for the pilots to offer a clue.

"Kitty Hawk Center…Kobold Two…do you copy?" Only static could be heard. "Kitty Hawk Center, this is Kobold Two…do you copy?"

He assumed several minutes had passed.

"Kobold Two…Kitty Hawk Center…Roger."

"Kitty Hawk…check…our feet are wet. Repeat…Our feet are wet."

"Roger…Kobold Two…copy that."

It confirmed in his mind they - Kobold Two - had crossed a shoreline below and were now flying toward their destination over water.

"Kitty Hawk…Kobold Two…how do you read?"

"Kobold Two…read you three…background static."

"Five by…Kobold Two…out."

He again tried to estimate the passage of time. All sounds about the chopper now changed. He sensed a downward motion, with less outside wind force, and a different engine making a quieter sound.

"Kitty Hawk Center…Kobold Two…with information India…ten miles south…three thousand five hundred feet…for landing."

Buffeting and turbulence increased.

"Kobold Two…pad one…wind one four at zero…cleared left downward…swell rise three feet…report final."

"Roger…Kitty Hawk Center…cleared left downward…one zero…report final…Kobold Two."

"Kitty Hawk Center…Kobold Two will perform three-sixty autorotation to one zero…pad one."

A pause in motion, and then he experienced a strong bounce. They had touched down. The headphones were taken from his head, but the hood remained. Two men, one on each side, guided him down from the chopper and onto the deck. As they moved away from the craft, one man pushed his head down to ensure his tall frame did not come in contact with the still whirling rotators.

The group ran across the landing pad to a hatch. They went through the hatch, down a passage, and arrived at what the prisoner presumed to be a room. He heard the lock open, and then they cut his bindings and removed the hood from his head. The door closed behind him. He heard it lock.

He found the room to be small and comfortable. On the only table in the room, he found a tray of real food and a bottle of fresh water. A feast for a man who had eaten only rice and water for as long as he could remember.

He discovered the room had access to a shower and toilet. He decided he would first shower and enjoy the meal, followed by sleep. After the shower, he dressed in a pair of tan slacks, a white golf shirt, and black running shoes.

Two days may have passed. He counted the meals and what they consisted of. He calculated three meals a day, an American custom. One was eggs and bacon: breakfast. He ate two breakfasts.

He heard a clunk at the door as the latch moved. They were coming to get him. A man ordered him to turn with his back to the door. He presumed this was so he would not see his captors. The bag was again placed over his head, although they did not bind him this time. They proceeded along a passageway. Another door opened. A person guided him to a chair. He sat down.

Next, belts were strapped across his body in an "X" configuration. Possibly fifteen minutes had passed.

A voice announced, "Ready?" A countdown began, "ten-nine-eight-seven…" It seemed to him they were going to launch him into outer space.

****

Two days later

He startled awake. Disorientated and dehydrated, he remained still, taking in his surroundings and assessing his personal status as well. It was a sunny day and warm day, and he assumed he was in a hotel room. The room lacked the ambiance of a typical Chinese room, prison, or ship's cabin. The room décor suggested a European motif.

For the time being, he felt too dizzy to move. He had a hangover but did not recall drinking alcohol. It would be best to lay on the bed until his brain developed some semblance of normality.

Further, he realized he was wearing an ensemble more typical of European attire, consisting of tan slacks, a white golf shirt and a pair of black loafers. He felt as though he had been out for the day and returned to this room and collapsed. Yet, his last recollection had him being kidnapped from Prison 2 in Beijing and flown to a ship.

It did not make any sense at all. Otherwise, he felt fine. He knew who he was, only not where he was. Or how he had gotten here. He felt strong enough to sit up. After taking a few deep breaths, he attempted to stand. Success! To walk would be the next big event. He crept to the window, from where he cast his gaze upon the street below. Yes, no mistaking it; the scene was somewhere in eastern Europe. His best guess was it was a large city, most likely Moscow or Saint Petersburg.

Working his way from the window back to the bed, he sat and once again scanned the room in search of a time reference. A call to whom he presumed to be the hotel's operator would solve the question. The call revealed the date, "Fifteen Oktober." Two weeks had elapsed since the Chinese prison.

By the following day, he believed he had recovered. He was back in Moscow, his home away from home. He arranged for several business meetings with former business partners and enough rubles to get him by until the following day.

Chapter 2

"Do we know what time she died?" Fay asked as her gaze swept the bedroom.

"No. The deceased's husband called us at 07:05, ma'am. When we arrived, we secured the area. We called the duty officer."

She turned to face Petty Officer Hadley. "Has anyone been in the home, other than you and Petty Officer Martin?" Fay asked.

"No one, Commander," came the reply.

"Let's keep it that way." Her gaze again surveyed the room. This was a woman's room, one decorated in pastels. Very tastefully done, very feminine, Fay thought. It would seem so perfect, if not for the woman who now lay dead on the bed before her. Her long red mane flowed like a stream across the satin floral print sheets and a crimson pillow covered her face. The late September morning sun highlighted her auburn locks as they spilled over the edge of the mattress, resembling a waterfall.

Fay sensed the presence of Death around her. In the curtains, in the book placed on the nightstand next to the bed. Even in the sunlight streaming through the window across the bed. Death lurked everywhere.

Although she had experienced Death before,

including three of her own near-death experiences, Navy Judge Advocate Commander Faydra Green had not gotten used to his genius. Then again, Death was not a person. Although he was, without a doubt, a man. His costume was complete with a giant sling blade and a black hooded cape shrouding his white, pasty face.

Those closest to her seemed to die. Her mother had died twenty-eight years before in an automobile accident. An accident had left her half-sister, JP Fletcher, injured and near death. Her father, former United States President William Green, had died a little over two years ago. And she had killed a man. Oh yes, Fay knew Death quite well.

Shaking off the lingering chill Death had left behind him in this once warm place, Fay instructed, "Okay, Hadley. Call the NCIS again. See if you can find out where my agent from the Special Assault Unit is. If they can't locate them, tell them I need anyone here now!"

"Aye, ma'am," he replied. The Shore Patrolman turned to leave the room.

"Hold up, Hadley. Where are the husband and the little girl?" Fay inquired.

"In the living room with Petty Officer Martin, ma'am."

Her cell phone rang. Withdrawing it from the right pocket of her winter jacket, she activated it and answered, "Fay Green. JAG Corps." She listened briefly and said in a dispassionate tone, "It's not pretty... it could be worse. Did you bring the bear?" She listened while the caller spoke. "See ya in a few."

She sighed and clicked off the phone, slipping it back into her pocket. "Petty Officer Fletcher will arrive in a few minutes," Fay informed Hadley. "You're looking for a tall woman, Hadley, with black hair. She'll be packing a teddy bear. Let her in. No one else gets in unless I say so."

"Aye, ma'am."

"And before you make the call, tell Mr. Caitlin I'll be out in a few minutes to speak to him."

Hadley nodded. He left the room.

Blessed with a photographic memory, Fay again scanned the bedroom, snapping mental snapshot after mental snapshot, her mind recording the death scene. The bedcovers were neat, unruffled, and tucked up under the deceased's chin. There was no sign she had struggled. A pair of slippers had been placed side by side on the floor near the bed, midway between the head and the foot, and were undisturbed. A bathrobe was draped over a chair set near the foot of the bed. She inhaled through her nostrils. The subtle scent of violets, perhaps?

Fay walked to the window, noting it to be latched; no broken glass. Glancing through the window, she observed a stand of firs growing tall in the park across the way. A man dressed in black stood in the lacy shadows just to the left of one of those trees; he was almost hidden from her view. He looked back at her. Fay felt her heart race; closing her eyes, she took a deep breath and clenched her teeth so hard a pain shot through her jaw. When she reopened her eyes, the man had disappeared. She turned away from the window. She knew him. And why he had come for her.

Considering the locked window, Fay reasoned whoever had entered this room had come and gone through the lone doorway. Glancing toward the door, her gaze shifted to the chest of drawers placed to the right. All of the drawers were closed; they too appeared to be undisturbed. A vase of one dozen red roses was placed on the chest. Robbery did not seem to be a motive.

Her gaze returned to the woman lying on the bed. The satin pillow covering her face troubled her. Why? Fay's head snapped back toward the chest. She revisited the flower arrangement; there was something odd about those roses. She approached the chest, stopping within reach of the bouquet. She studied the flowers, counting each crimson bud. There were eleven flowers, not the customary twelve.

Returning to the bed, she sank to her knees and leaned forward so she could view the hardwood floor beneath. There was not so much as a dust mite evident. Fay glanced up at the corpse lying not more than three feet from her. "You got the housekeeping approval award, darlin'," she whispered to the corpse. "You were a better woman than me."

As she rose to her feet, Fay glanced at the deceased's left foot protruding from beneath the bedcovers. Noticing several minor red abrasions on the skin near the heel, she drew her face nearby. Had the woman nicked herself while shaving her legs, perhaps?

Closer examination revealed three distinct abrasions. It appeared the woman had been bitten. The largest and most distinct abrasion resembled the letter "J." Bringing the tip of her right index finger up and touching her own left breast, Fay recalled a similar mark residing there. Hers was a constant reminder of a savage rape and beating she had endured some years ago. Her attacker had bitten her; the "J" shaped scar, the result of his bite, remained today. This memory caused her to pause. She sighed and stood.

Glancing at her wristwatch, she noted five minutes

had passed. Refreshing her lungs with a deep breath of air, Fay turned away from the bed and left the room. As she passed from the bedroom into the hallway leading toward the living room, she worked at removing the latex gloves from her moist, trembling hands. She was just slipping the gloves into the left and right pockets of her full-length, black leather winter coat as Petty Officer J. Fletcher entered the small living room through the front door.

A soft and straightforward nod from Fay acknowledged JP's presence. "Hey," Fay offered. This was a greeting that would, more often than not, be accompanied by enthusiasm and a warm smile. But not this day.

With her heart lodged in her throat, she approached Marine Sergeant Caitlin and his daughter. Father and daughter sat hand in hand on a forest green, soft leather sofa.

Making eye contact with the girl, Fay said, "Hi, honey." She sank to her knees in front of the girl.

The girl seemed unruffled; she was not yet aware her mother lay dead in the next room.

Fay extended her right hand toward the girl. "I'm Faydra. What's your name, honey?"

The girl smiled. "Abigail," she said in a soft, shy voice; she extended her right hand to grasp Fay's hand.

Commander Green held the small hand, thinking how millions of tiny hands like Abigail's would grow to one day grasp the future. This future, regrettably, would not include her mother. Fay revitalized her fortitude. "Abigail is a nice name," she replied. "How old are you, sweetheart?"

Abigail held up her left hand, displaying four

15

fingers. "Five." She added, "My mommy is sleeping. Can I go wake her up?"

"Not now, sweetie." Fay smiled. Her voice unwavering, she said, "When I was five, I had pretty blonde hair and dazzling green eyes, like yours!"

Abigail giggled.

"Sweetheart, I need to talk to your daddy for a few minutes. Would it be okay with you?" Fay asked the little girl.

Abigail nodded, yes.

Fay pointed toward Petty Officer Fletcher, who smiled and held out the teddy bear so Abigail could better see it. "The nice lady over there is Petty Officer Fletcher. You can call her JP. She's a real nice lady. I know because JP is my sister," Fay explained.

Abigail's gaze locked in on the bear. She nodded her head as Fay spoke.

"Would you like to go with her while I talk to your daddy?" Fay asked.

Abigail hopped down from the sofa and rushed toward JP. JP sank to her knees and offered the teddy bear to the girl.

Fay watched while Abigail hugged the large black and white bear. Fay asked, "Abigail, would you and your bear like to go outside with JP? I bet you could talk her into taking you for some ice cream. Would you like that?"

Clutching the great bear in her arms, the girl looked toward her father, her large green eyes seeking his consent.

"Go with Petty Officer Fletcher, Abby," he encouraged.

Fay waited until JP and Abigail had departed

through the entry door; then, she turned back toward the Marine. She rose to her feet, walked a few steps to the sofa, and sat at the opposite end from him.

Shore Patrolman Hadley entered the room via the front entry door. "Excuse me, ma'am," he said. "Agent Corry Markham from the NCIS has been located. He's on his way."

"Thank you, Mr. Hadley."

Fay's gaze followed Petty Officer Hadley as he left the room. She turned her attention to the Marine. "Mr. Caitlin, I'm here because the duty officer could not locate the Navy Criminal Investigative Service special agent," she began. "They found me instead. I understand he has been located, so I'm going to bow out." She forced a smile. "As a judge advocate, let me give you some advice."

The Marine gave a thankful nod and remained silent.

"I don't know what happened here, nor will I presume anything, for that matter," Fay went on. "The Special Agent will have some questions for you. Article 31 of the Uniform Code of Military Justice affords you specific rights. You do have the right to remain silent. It means you have the right to say nothing at all. Listen to what Mr. Markham has to say," she cautioned. "Remember, he is on your side, as am I. You, of course, will want to cooperate with him. Any statement you make, either oral or written, can be used against you in a trial by court-martial. He will say you have a right to counsel, either by a military lawyer or by a civilian lawyer. You can request a lawyer be present during any interview." Fay conveyed a sympathetic smile to the Marine. "Understood?"

"Yes, ma'am."

"I know this is tough. I promise we will get through this, David."

Caitlin nodded.

"Do you have any family living in the area?" Fay inquired.

"I have a sister who lives in Oregon."

"What is her name?"

"Debbie Owens," Caitlin replied.

"I suggest you contact Debbie Owens when you've finished speaking to Mr. Markham." Fay looked toward the entry door. "Considering Abigail, you're going to need your sister's help." She returned her gaze to the Marine. As she did, she slipped her hand into her right pocket and withdrew one of her business cards. "Here's my card. Call me if you need me."

The Marine accepted the card, studied it, and responded, "Thank you, ma'am."

"Sergeant, the roses on the dresser are beautiful. Is it a birthday or an anniversary?" Fay asked him.

"No. I was happy to see my wife after returning home from a mission. So, I got her a dozen roses," Caitlin replied. "I will refresh those next week."

"One dozen?" Fay asked. She recalled counting eleven.

"Yes, ma'am. A dozen."

The entry door opened. Petty Officer Hadley reentered the room, his expression conveying a sense of urgency. "Ma'am. Can I see you outside for a minute?" he asked.

****

08:50 hours, home of Marine Sergeant Adams

"When did you last see your wife alive?"

"Last night, ma'am." The Marine shrugged his

broad shoulders. "We'd been drinkin' wine. We went to bed early. We watched TV. I fell asleep." He again shrugged his shoulders. "That's about it."

"Do you recall the time, Sergeant Adams?" Fay asked.

He thought. "I can't say. It must have been around 00:30?" he guessed.

"Was she alive at 00:30?"

"Yes, ma'am. I know 'cause Candy had a bitch about something. I looked at the clock, listened to her bitch for a while longer." He shook his head in disbelief. "Next thing I know, it was mornin'."

"How long have you two been married?" Fay inquired.

"Two years, three months."

"Were you having marital problems?" she asked next.

"I didn't think so."

Fay wrinkled her brow. "You didn't think so?"

"We were happy before I left for my tour in Asia," Adams explained. "When I got back, she told me she wanted a divorce."

Fay frowned. "This surprised you?"

"Blindsided me would be a better choice of words, ma'am," Adams responded.

"Do you have any children, Mr. Adams?"

"None. We talked about tryin' for some. Until this divorce bullshit came up."

"Mr. Adams," Fay admonished.

"Sorry, ma'am. I'm just confused right now."

"You have returned home from a duty assignment, and you are now on leave?" she continued.

"Yes, ma'am."

"Where were you stationed?"

"I am with a special forces unit; the mission is classified," Adams explained.

"I am sorry for asking," Fay replied. Fay knew by his response she could not pry any further.

"I tell you what, Julio." Fay handed Sergeant Adams her card. "If you need me, I want you to call me. Okay?"

Adams smiled. "I will for sure, ma'am. Thank you."

Fay also reasoned because Special Agent Markham was tied up with Sergeant Caitlin, it would be some time before Markham got around to Julio Adams. She needed to get him away from the home while Candy's body was relocated to either the morgue or the base hospital.

"Sergeant, do you have family in the area?" Fay asked.

"No, ma'am."

"Unfortunately, this is now a crime scene. I want to get you into base housing for a few days while we work on the preliminaries of an investigation," Fay said. "And then you can come back. Do you mind?"

"No, ma'am. I think I would appreciate it."

"Okay. I will have the shore patrolman escort you to the base housing administrator. I want you to keep me posted as to where you are," Fay instructed.

"I will do, ma'am."

****

09:55 hours, home of Marine Sergeant Main

"You mentioned you and your wife were having marital problems."

"Yes, ma'am. I found out she had had an affair."

Fay referred to her notebook. "The affair began before you left for your tour in Asia, is that correct, Sergeant Main?" she asked.

"It's not the first time, Commander."

"First time for what?"

"She was a slut when I married her and a slut when she died. I should have known she would cheat on me, but I thought marriage would change her," Main responded.

"People often don't change, Sergeant."

"I think I know now."

"How many other men were there?" Fay asked.

"Lisa was a stripper. Who knows? There could have been hundreds."

"I would assume you know Sergeant Caitlin?" Fay guessed.

"I do. We just did our last tour together," Main answered. "And as you know, he and his wife occupy the other half of this duplex."

"The NCIS will conduct an investigation into Lisa's death. And, as I alluded to earlier, you can expect to be interviewed by an NCIS special agent." Commander Green glanced at her watch. "I need to report to the duty officer," she went on. "He'll get you a room in the temporary duty barracks. Your home is now a crime scene. You can't come back here. Understood?"

"Aye, ma'am."

Fay offered Sergeant Main her card. "Jody, I want you to call me. We can work through this together. Okay?"

Jody smiled. "For sure, Commander."

Chapter 3

"SHIP DEAD AHEAD, CAPTAIN!" the lookout yelled.

"FULL STARBOARD RUDDER! ALL ENGINES FULL!" the captain ordered.

"Right full rudder, aye. All full," the quartermaster confirmed.

She watched, feeling powerless as the dark superstructure loomed before her. She knew this ship.

As the ship drew closer, she tightened her jaw and braced for the collision. "WE'RE GOING TO RAM HER!" she screamed as she woke from her dream.

She sat up in her bed. The early morning sunlight trickled in through the curtain drawn across her bedroom window. She reached for the glass of water she had placed on the nightstand at the left of her bed. Russian? Good Lord.

****

08:00 hours, Monday, NCIS Northwest Regional Office, Silverdale, Washington

"Thank you for stopping by, ladies."

Commander Green and Petty Officer J. Fletcher sat across the desk from NCIS Special Agent Corry Markham.

"Not a problem," Fay replied. "You're located between where I live and JAG Corps. This seemed easier." Fay turned to JP. "This is my Legalman, Mrs. JP

Fletcher. She will record our conversation this morning."

Markham smiled at JP. Petty Officer Fletcher returned the smile; she retrieved her tablet from the black canvas carrying case near her feet.

Markham returned his attention to Fay. "I understand the Convening Authority has ordered JAG Corps to assist us in our investigation," he stated.

"That's correct. The CA has requested we conduct a JAGMAN investigation to run concurrently with yours," Fay confirmed. "I'm here to assure you JAG Corps will not interfere with the NCIS investigation and to minimize duplication of effort."

Markham offered a hapless grin. "I've got three murders to investigate, Commander. I'll take any help I can get." He paused. His eyes brightened. "Would either of you like a cup of coffee? Or tea?"

Fay smiled. "Coffee. Black would be fine."

"Tea, please," Petty Officer Fletcher said.

"I could use a strong coffee myself." Markham stood. "Sit tight. I'll be back." He left the office.

"What do you think?" Fay asked JP as she watched the office door close behind Markham.

"When prepared for worse, can hope for best."

"Chan?" Fay asked.

JP nodded. "Chan."

Fay smiled. "Continue, JP."

JP shifted in her chair. "I'd hate to be in Mr. Markham's shoes right now," she whispered.

"You're right. One death investigation is stressful enough. To investigate three… well, I'd find it rather difficult."

"Excuse me, ma'am," JP interrupted. "You too have three deaths to investigate."

Fay frowned. "True," she mused. "What do we know about Corry Markham?"

Petty Officer Fletcher turned her attention to her tablet. Her gaze scanned the screen. Looking up at Fay, she commented, "He played football at the Naval Academy."

"Annapolis? He's a civilian. What happened?"

"He dropped out in his senior year." JP referred to her computer notes. "Says he went to work for the NCIS."

"No kidding? Interesting." Fay glanced at the office door. "Regarding the football, what position did he play?" she asked.

"Don't know. I'd say, based on his size, probably not a lineman," JP speculated.

"He's too small, right?"

"Your lack of knowledge of the game, ma'am, is only eclipsed by your beauty," JP replied teasingly. "But…yeah. Not enough beef."

"I'm a blonde!" Fay exclaimed. "Give me a break!" A soft smile formed on her lips. "A quarterback, perhaps?"

"I don't recall the Middies havin' an African-American quarterback around the time Mr. Markham would have attended the Academy," JP replied.

"Perhaps a running back, JP, or a defensive back?" Fay posited. "I suppose we could ask him."

"Wanna bet lunch he played runnin' back?"

"Ok," Fay agreed. "I'll guess defensive back."

"Whatever position he played," JP said, "I do know when I looked into his eyes a few minutes ago he had the 'deer caught in the headlights' look in them."

Fay sighed. "This is a tough one. I keep thinking

about the little girl."

"Abigail?"

Fay nodded. "She reminds me of me when I was her age."

"She's a dead ringer for you when you were her age, ma'am," JP observed.

"Sad." Fay's face brightened, but then, she frowned. "You were about her age when your birth mom died."

"Well, more like two." JP sighed. "I had yet to comprehend the concept of death. I do recall I kept wonderin' where she went to. People kept sayin' she went to heaven. And I kept askin', 'When will she be back?'"

Fay sat silently for a minute. Then she said, "You seemed to be a pretty sensitive kid when you were two years old."

"So true," JP confirmed with a solemn nod. "It was even harder for me to understand when our mom died. To me, the woman who adopted me was my real mom. That one was tough."

Fay sniffed. A single tear formed in the corner of each of her almond-shaped, sea-green eyes. "I know. I miss her so much." Her gaze met her sister's. "How'd we get onto this topic, anyway?" Fay asked as she brushed away the tears with the tip of her right index finger.

"It's the case, ma'am. It and the little girl." Petty Officer Fletcher glanced toward the door. "What's keepin' Mr. Markham? He only went for coffee."

"I suppose not a running back," Fay joked.

Corry Markham reentered the office, carrying a plastic tray with three Styrofoam cups placed on it. Fay did not notice it at first, but then she spotted a small brown stain on the left pocket of his white shirt.

Markham placed the small plastic tray and cups on his desk, removed a handkerchief from his right trouser pocket, and brushed at the brown stain. With a sheepish look on his face, he said, "I ran into someone in the hall. Literally!" He smiled and shook his head. "I suppose it could have been worse." He handed each woman her beverage. "I did manage to save most of it."

Fay and JP accepted their cups, and in unison, said, "Thanks."

Markham smiled and sat down.

Fay sipped at her coffee and said, "JP tells me you played ball at the Academy, Mr. Markham."

A broad smile formed on his face. He shifted his gaze from Fay to JP. "I did! Are you a Middies fan, JP?"

"I used to be," Fletcher replied. "My dad was a Midshipman."

Corry's eyes again brightened. "That's right! He did play ball for the Academy. In fact, I had the pleasure of meeting your father."

"Oh? How so?" Fay asked.

"He spoke at the commencement ceremony during my junior year, Commander."

"Yes, it would have been the year before our father passed," Fay estimated.

Markham's expression saddened. His voice softened. "The nation lost a great man when your father died." All were silent. "It must be an honor for you ladies to have one of the Navy's largest aircraft carriers bear your family name."

"One would think," Fay responded. "JP and I were both at the christening of the U.S.S. *William Green*. I have not set foot on her since. Too many memories." A small tear again formed in the corner of her left eye. She brushed it away with the tip of her left index finger. Refreshing her smile, she went on, "I have a question for you, Mr. Markham."

"Go for it," he replied.

"While you were away, my sister and I were speculating about which position you might have played when you attended the Academy," Fay told him.

"Running back," Markham answered. His ego seemed to swell. The tone of his voice strengthened. "In fact, I'm in the process of trying to decide whether to continue my career with the NCIS or to play pro football."

"You still have a choice whether or not to play pro ball?" Fay asked.

"Three years is not a long time, Commander. I'm still in great shape."

"I'd bet would be a tough choice," JP said.

"Yes, it is," Markham said. "I think I've found a home here." He glanced around the office. His expression conveyed the look of a distant dream. "The fame and the fortune pro ball would afford me and my family would be nice too."

Fay smiled. Time to get back to the business at hand. "I'm sure, when the time comes, Mr. Markham, your decision will be the one which makes the most sense to you." Fay sipped at her coffee. As she placed her cup on the desk in front of her, her expression hardened. "Other than the investigation being conducted by the NCIS," she continued, "I'm here to ascertain if the three deaths might also be under investigation by either the FBI or by local civilian law enforcement."

"As you know, the deaths of Candy Adams, Lisa Main, and Marina Caitlin all occurred on a military reservation," Markham told her. "At this time, as far as I know, no other agencies are or will be involved."

"Thank you," Fay replied. "To maximize cooperation, I'll be responsible for coordinating the JAG Corps' investigation with yours. By working together, we can complete both investigations."

"Not a problem, Commander."

Fay sipped at her coffee, then returned the cup to the desk. "I'll direct our JAGMAN investigators to communicate and coordinate their investigation with you. I'll add the appropriate language to the convening order. I don't anticipate any conflicts arising between the Convening Authority and the NCIS."

Markham shook his head from side to side. "I don't foresee us having any problems either," he corroborated.

"If you should have any objection to our investigation or to a particular aspect of our investigation, tell me," Fay requested. "Be assured the CA will suspend the contested action pending his resolution."

Markham smiled. "Standard procedure, Commander."

"Good," Fay replied. "I look forward to working with you, Mr. Markham." She sighed. "Thank goodness only one child is involved."

A hint of doubt came to his face. "Two, ma'am."

"What? Two?" Fay asked.

"Abigail has a sister."

"I didn't know," Fay replied, her voice reflecting her surprise. "Older or younger?"

"She's older."

Fay shifted her gaze from Markham to JP, then back to Markham. "Where is the girl now?"

"She's visiting with her biological father and his wife in Idaho," Markham explained.

Fay again glanced at Petty Officer Fletcher. "A half-sister."

Special Agent Markham referred to his notes. "Correct, ma'am. Her name is Jenny. Jenny is ten years old."

Fay spoke to no one in particular. "It just doesn't get any easier, does it?" She shook her head in disbelief. "My God." In a stronger voice, she said, "I'll have someone from the Chaplain Corps visit Jenny and her father."

Chapter 4

On a warm late March afternoon, two men met in an open-air café on Moscow's pedestrian-only Old Arbat Street. The two men found it a peaceful place to conduct their business. Both men conversed in hushed tones. Their eyes did not meet as they spoke to one another. When their conversation concluded, one man handed the other man a photograph.

"Faye King," Roman Justine said.

"Faye King," Evilenko wrote on the back of the photo.

****

NCIS Special Agent Corry Markham spent his morning reviewing the three dead women's coroner reports, looking for a link - anything that might tie one case to the other. Two of the women, Marina Caitlin and Lisa Main, had been strangled; the third woman had drowned in her bathtub. When he considered the preliminary evidence, he had no suspect. Any one, or all, of the three women's husbands could have killed them. Perhaps he would learn more when he interviewed each of the men later within the next two days.

Corry placed the three reports on his desk and rocked back in his chair. Placing his hands behind his head, he closed his eyes. As he reviewed each file, he wondered if perhaps one person might have murdered all three women.

Cindy Adams's husband had found her body in a bathtub half full of water. Her lungs had been filled with water. There did not seem to have been a struggle. A possible explanation would be she had either been drugged or had become inebriated. He made a note to have the coroner focus on those options.

Marina Caitlin had died while she had slept in her bed. She had not fought for her life. It was as if both women had willfully succumbed to death. Again, was she drugged or inebriated?

On the other hand, Lisa Main had fought her attacker. Her body had been found on the living room floor; she, too, had been strangled. Evidence suggested Lisa had put up a fight. Death had not claimed her easily. *Good for you, girl*, he thought. *At least you went out fighting.* Did Sergeant Main display any markings consistent with of an altercation?

****

7:10 A.M., Silverdale, Washington

Fay sipped at a cup of her favorite local brew, Seattle's Best Coffee. No day could begin without at least two cups, strong and black. She listened to the local new station's television coverage of the significant Pacific Rim Security Agreement talks underway in nearby Seattle. World leaders from Japan, South Korea, China, Canada, Mexico, Russia, and the United States had convened to discuss and sign this historic pact. There was tight security, according to the report. Although several thousand protesters had assembled on the streets of downtown Seattle, the protests were, for the time being, peaceful.

In a few hours, she and her sister would travel to Seattle to attend a party given by the governor of

Washington State in honor of the President of the United States, Armand Ross. It had been a few years since Fay had last seen Armand; she looked forward to the party. Two of her friends, Korean President Lee Ka-Eun and her advisor, Jangho Kim, would be in town. She hoped she would have an opportunity to meet with them as well.

As she listened to the news broadcast, Fay scanned the Seattle Post's website. She found a small article, buried near the back of the "A" section, reporting the deaths of the three Bremerton area women. She read the Seattle pro baseball team was headed for the American League Championship playoff series this year for a change. Coach Wells praised his overachieving players. The weather report forecast rain for the next three days, while her horoscope predicted unexpected travel. All in all, pretty dull stuff.

Fay picked up a small container of fish food. She tapped a small portion of food into the aquarium housing her pet guppy, Joey. She had learned early on guppies were like rabbits. So, while Joey had originally been going it alone, she hadn't wanted him to be lonely and had gotten him a little buddy: a catfish she had named him (her, it?) Garfield.

The sharp chime of her cell interrupted her morning solitude. Thinking it might be JP, Fay answered with a cheerful, "Mornin'!" Several minutes later, she clicked off the cell and proceeded to fling, with more force than she intended, the first object her hand could grasp.

As the small cookbook ricocheted off of one of the kitchen cabinets, she screamed, "GOD DAMN IT! MOTHER OF A BITCH!" Was there a foul phrase greater than "pissed?" She didn't know it.

****

Fay often liked to walk, content to be alone with her thoughts. Occasionally, she would talk to herself, contemplate a problem, worry about something or someone. She found this her time to daydream, to wonder why things did not occur as she had planned them to be.

Kicking at a rock, stopping to pet a dog, or feeding a peanut to a squirrel - sometimes, when very angry, she did not notice any of these things. She did not even notice the rain.

A damp breeze persisted; it seemed spring was struggling to get itself started. The water-soaked sidewalk gleamed wet and black. Otherwise, it was a terrible day darkened by rain clouds, one that left her soul cold, chilled with anxiety. All in all, the typical crummy Pacific Northwest day.

Thunder rolled across the sky. Flipping up the collar of her raincoat, keeping her chin tucked down, and pulling low her uniform hat, from which the rain poured in streams, Fay jammed her hands down into the warmth of her coat pockets and slogged on.

Soon she stopped at a wooden park bench, dark and swollen with moisture, and sat down. A woman scolded her child as the two hurried by; Fay wondered what dreadful thing the child could have done to invoke such rage in her mother. Every action had an equal and opposite reaction. Love turned to hate. People snapped; sometimes, they killed. It was all about the children, wasn't it? Children like Abigail and her sister, Jenny. It was not fair.

Someone sat down on the bench next to her. She knew him. He held an umbrella in his right hand, yet Fay did not acknowledge him. The man pressed the umbrella toward her. The raindrops ceased to shower her head.

She sat silently before she spoke. "There's room for two under here, Mr. Markham. Scoot over."

He did. The sound of the rain drumming on the umbrella was the only sound she heard.

"Petty Officer Fletcher said you were out here," Markham informed her. "I've been walking behind you for about ten minutes."

"I know, Mr. Markham. Just me and my shadow," Fay said as she glanced in the direction she thought she had last seen the man dressed in black. "I thought if I did not stop walking, you would not catch me."

"You do move pretty fast, ma'am."

"I move fast when I am annoyed." Grasping the umbrella's handle and taking it from Corry Markham, Fay stood. "My ass is getting wet. Walk with me."

There were several more minutes of silence as the two people walked in the rain. Fay spoke first. "When I was a child, Mr. Markham, my mother told me I was a thoroughbred," she began. "I protested, 'Mama, I am not a horse!' My mother laughed and replied, 'No, Darlin'. It means y'all have spirit.' You see, sir, my mother was a true Southern lady. A belle in every sense of the word. At the time, I did not appreciate her concept. As I grew, I came to know what courage and strength truly were."

Fay stopped walking. Without looking in Corry's direction, she said, "I can assure you, Mr. Markham, I once had more than my fair share of spirit."

She again began to walk. "Several years ago, a man, a man I loved, gave his life in an attempt to protect me from a man who had beaten and raped me. I later killed him. They said it was in self-defense. Yet, even today,

I'm not so sure. Following the incident, my father died. One morning, I awoke to realize I had lost my spirit. I was no longer a thoroughbred. Now I do what I have to do. I'm ashamed to say I no longer find passion in my purpose." Fay turned her head toward Corry Markham and asked, "So, how's your day?"

"I thought it urgent I talked to you. Now…I'm not so sure," Markham admitted.

Fay smiled. "Oh, don't mind me. Like I said, I have managed to achieve a high level of 'piss-a-tivity' for the moment."

A look of concern formed on Corry's face. "Anything you care to talk about, ma'am?"

She did not reply.

"You've got long legs, Commander," Markham observed as he tried to keep pace with her.

"Says the running back at the Academy." Fay slowed her pace. "Sorry. I did ask you to walk with me." She continued to walk. "I find myself adrift of late, Mr. Markham. Those spirited battles I once fought with such courage, commitment, and determination now seem futile to me. My pragmatism seems to have replaced my courage, while my commitment and my determination are nowhere to be found."

Markham seemed to consider her words and then said, "I received the preliminary autopsy reports from the coroner this morning."

Fay thought back, recalling her visual surveillance of each of the three crime scenes. "Candy Adams drowned in her bath. Lisa Main was strangled, and Marina Caitlin was suffocated with a pillow from her bed," she recounted.

"No," Markham revealed. "Marina Caitlin was also

strangled."

Fay stopped. Drops of rain dripped from the ends of her blonde hair. She brushed a large raindrop from the tip of her nose with a swipe of her left hand and sniffed. "What?" she asked, with a look of disbelief evident on her face. "A pillow covered Marina's face. How did she get strangled? Did she have bruises on her neck?"

Markham nodded. "Each woman had been bitten on her neck and breast."

Fay stopped short. Her attacker had also bitten her on the breast and neck. Yet, it was a different place and a different time. "Crap. That's all I need right now," she responded. She began walking again. "Do any of the husbands have an alibi?"

"Adams was passed out in bed when his wife drowned in her bath. Main was out driving, alone, when his wife died."

"And Mr. Caitlin?" Fay inquired.

"Caitlin claims he was drinking beer with God at the Pollywog bar."

"God, you say?"

"The Lord God Almighty," Markham confirmed.

"Mercy. What were they talking about?" Fay asked. "I suppose it doesn't matter now. I'm off the case."

"Ma'am?" Markham asked, confused.

"About two hours ago, I received a phone call from Admiral Brandon May."

"May? You know him?" Markham asked.

"Yep," Fay replied. "But FYI, May is Special Operations Warfare Command. I have been reassigned to two weeks' temporary duty aboard the U.S.S. *William Green*. Captain Vern Towsley, JAG Corps will replace me on this investigation."

"Carrier JAG is a plum assignment, ma'am."

"Agreed. A plum for any JA to serve on a carrier. Except for me on board the *William Green*. As I said before, there are too many painful memories associated with the ship." Fay sighed. "I had hoped to one day watch the sunrise at Khufu, to walk the forest of a New England fall, and to view Kilimanjaro from across the Serengeti, all before I set foot aboard the U.S.S. *William Green*, Mr. Markham. I fly out tomorrow night. Tonight, I am to attend a Governor's Ball in honor of President Ross."

Chapter 5

She chatted with Senator Kennedy. She recalled a fifth-generation Kennedy, yet this one was a Republican, as odd as it seemed to her. She knew one thing for sure - Republican or no, the married senator was hitting on her. Yes, the senator was still a Kennedy. Fay continued to smile and chat, until someone approached her from behind and touched her shoulder. Excusing herself, she turned.

"Excuse me, Miss Green. Is important," a tall woman with auburn hair whispered.

Saved at last! She turned back to Senator Kennedy, and with a pleading look, Fay asked, "Will you please excuse me, Senator?"

"Of course," she replied.

The tall woman placed her right index finger to her lips. "I am Irena. You must now come with me."

Fay followed the tall, athletic woman from the ballroom while trying to discreetly signal her sister she was leaving the party. Fay did not know if she was successful or not.

When the two women reached a service door, Irena hesitated. Still whispering, she said, "You will speak only when spoken to. When meeting is concluded, you will return to party and will not speak of meeting to anyone."

Fay reasoned the woman's accent was Eastern European. She replied, "I understand."

Irena smiled as she drew open the door. Fay passed through the door and into a service hall leading from the ballroom toward the catering kitchen. She waited while Irena closed the door behind them.

"Come," Irena said, and the two women proceeded along the hallway, dotted with Secret Service personnel, toward the kitchen.

No one challenged them, and now Fay realized her escort was most likely a Russian Secret Service agent. She knew she would be meeting with someone of importance.

The two women passed through the busy catering kitchen, arriving at a door located at the back of the kitchen. "Catering Manager," the sign on the door read. Irena opened the door and motioned for Fay to enter the office.

"Commander Green," Irena announced to the two men seated in the small and dingy office. One of the men sat behind the cluttered desk, the other in front of it.

President Ross! President Rudkovsky! Fay masked her shock as she extended her hand toward the man she knew well. "President Ross. Good to see you again, sir," she said.

"Commander Green," Ross replied as he rose from his chair.

Fay shifted her gaze to her left, smiled and spoke. "Mr. Rudkovsky, *rada poznakomitsya*." *("Nice to meet you.")*

The President of Russia smiled and rose from his chair. "*Horosho. Spasibo*. Likewise, Commander Green," he said in greeting. "My friend here has told me much about you."

"All good, I hope, Mr. President," Fay replied.

"All good, I assure you, Commander," Rudkovsky said. He smiled again and then asked, "You speak Russian?"

"*Sovsem nemnogo.* Not so much, sir. You can call me Fay, Mr. President," she responded with a hopeful expression on her face.

"Fay it is," Rudkovsky replied.

President Ross motioned toward the remaining vacant chair facing him. "Please, Fay. Join us," he said.

Fay complied with his wish by sitting down.

President Armand Ross had served as Vice President during her father's two terms in office. He had returned to the Senate, only to return to the White House ten years later to serve. Mrs. Ross had delivered the eulogy at Fay's father's funeral.

There were many questions on her mind. Foremost, why were the President of the United States and the President of Russia sitting in a dingy catering office, as if they were two boys who had managed to sneak away from a boring party only to loosen their neckties to enjoy a good cigar and a shot of whiskey? She knew this would not be a social visit. Remembering Irena's warning - "speak only if spoken to" - she remained silent.

"Can I offer you a cup of coffee, Fay?" President Ross asked. "Or a shot of whiskey, perhaps?"

Fay smiled and nodded. "Coffee would be perfect, sir." She reconsidered, adding, "With a shot of whisky, sir."

Ross turned to President Rudkovsky. "Coffee, Yuri?"

He nodded, yes. "And I too for the whiskey. It is

American, yes?"

Yuri Rudkovsky spoke to Irena in Russian. She acknowledged him with a simple nod, turned, and left the room. His gaze followed the vivacious woman as she departed through the door.

President Ross asked, "How have you been, Faydra?"

"Not too bad, sir. I had a rough time of it when Dad died. But of late, things seem to be on the upswing," she lied. "How about you, sir?"

Ross shook his head from side to side. "I sometimes wonder why I ever chose a life in politics." He touched the top of his head with his right hand. "This white hair used to be black. Not so four years ago!"

"I know, sir. My father had a similar experience," Fay recounted.

The constant smile on Ross's lips faded. "Faydra." He glanced at President Rudkovsky. "Yuri and I have a problem," he stated. "One I think you can help us solve."

She felt her throat tighten.

"Two weeks ago, an American Navy vessel collided with a Russian Navy vessel," Ross went on. "Unfortunately, several politicians from both sides got involved and pushed for a full-blown investigation. The result could lead to the court-martials of both captains and a hell of a lot of press we would just as soon not have." He stopped talking when Irena returned with the coffee service.

After she finished serving the coffee, Irena headed for the door.

"Irena," Rudkovsky called after her, "you must remain. We will need you as well." As if he were reminding her of something, he said, "Evilenko,

Irishka."

Irena nodded as she turned back toward the three people. Remaining motionless, she stood with her hands clasped in front of her.

Ross continued. "Either our American captain was negligent, or our Russian captain was negligent."

"Or sir…" Fay hesitated. "Or neither captain was negligent."

A knowing grin formed on Ross's lips. He again glanced toward Rudkovsky, who also grinned. Returning his gaze to Fay, Ross said, "You said it, Faydra, not me."

"Yes, sir. I did."

"The Navy Mishap Board has completed its investigation and has made its recommendations. A court of inquiry will commence aboard the *William Green* within the week."

"And this is why I have been assigned to a green table aboard the *Green*, sir?" Fay asked.

"The court, or green table as you call it, will consist of two admirals from the American side and an admiral and a captain from the Russian side," Ross explained. "You will occupy the fifth chair as legal on behalf of JAG Corps."

"Sir, my background is in international law, not maritime law," Fay reminded him.

"Close enough, Commander. From the Russian side, Captain Alexander Lavrov is a lawyer who is well versed in maritime law. You can rely on his expertise, as he will yours."

"Thank you, sir."

Ross smiled. "I know you will do what's right, Faydra."

"I know I will, sir," she replied.

"One more thing." Ross leaned toward her. In a whisper, he said, "During the inquiry, you may hear something a bit out of the ordinary. Keep an open mind." He sat back in his seat.

"Sir?"

Ross continued to smile. "Thank you, Faydra."

Fay returned to the party, wondering what President Ross had meant by "out of the ordinary." And what was an "Evilenko?" And what part in this would Irena play?

Fay found her sister.

JP asked, "Where were y'all?"

Fay nodded toward the service entrance. "Restroom."

"Mercy, woman! That was like twenty minutes ago!"

"I really needed to go, darlin'."

"No kidding! Are you alright?" her sister asked.

"Just fine!"

"How'd yer meetin' go?"

"What meeting?"

JP lowered her voice to a whisper. "With President Ross."

"How…?" Fay asked, her voice trailing off.

"I know all…I see all," JP deadpanned. "To be truthful, I spotted you just as you disappeared through the service entrance with Natasha."

"Natasha?"

"The Russian woman," her sister replied. "You know. Natasha and Boris? The two dimwitted spies on the *Rocky and Bullwinkle Show*?"

"Oh, yeah."

"When you didn't come back, I tried to follow you." JP pointed toward the door. "I made it as far as the door, and Bill Bennett appeared from out of thin air and stopped me."

"Bill Bennett, from the Secret Service?" Fay asked. "I would have thought he had retired years ago!"

"I guess not. It was Bill," JP confirmed. "Anyway, we was chattin', and he told me you was meetin' with President Ross. So that's how I knew."

"Did he say anything else?"

"No. I think myself lucky to have wormed that much out of him," JP said with a sly grin. "He remembered my Secret Service code name."

"Energy!" Fay recalled.

"Yeah."

"All I can tell you is we are to take part in a green table aboard the U.S.S. *Green*," Fay said. It was time to change the subject. "I had another dream last night," she went on.

"Roman Justine?" her sister guessed.

"Yeah," Fay confirmed. "The dreams are becoming more frequent."

"The doctor told you the dreams are brought on by stress."

"Our visiting the U.S.S. *Green* is stressful enough for me, not to mention the three murders."

"The same dream?" JP asked. "The one where you kill him?"

"Yeah."

"Can we talk about this later?" JP requested, pointing toward the other side of the room. "There is something waiting that is guaranteed to cheer you up."

"Great!" Fay exclaimed. "I can use it."

"President Lee and Jangho have been waiting to see you."

"Who am I to keep the President of Korea and her attaché waiting? Let's go say hello!" Fay declared.

Shortly past midnight, Fay and JP bid farewell to President Lee and Colonel Jangho Kim. They were faced with a two-hour trek home, providing the ferry schedule offered early morning service. Fay knew it would be impossible to find a vacant hotel room in the city because of the Pacific Rim Conference. As she had suspected, the woman at the Four Seasons reception confirmed there was not a room in the city to be had - unless you could name drop President of the United States Armand Ross, President of Korea Lee Ka-Eun, and former President of the United States William Green. If one could do that, then one could have a nonexistent room, just for the taking. Fay and JP were given an incredible suite on the top floor of the Four Seasons. No charge!

****

The Caitlin house was dark. Removing a small flashlight from her left coat pocket, Fay clicked it on. With her free right hand, she cleared away the yellow police line barrier tape blocking the door. She tested the doorknob. The unlocked door opened, and she pushed her way into the living room. The house was silent except for the ticking of a clock, which she could not see. Pausing to gain her bearings, she moved forward. The sound of her boot heels clicking on the hardwood floor echoed as she proceeded toward the bedroom located at the back of the house. Her right index finger found the trigger of the derringer located in her coat pocket. *Deja vu. I've been here before.*

Hearing a noise behind her, Fay snapped off the flashlight. In one fluid motion, she spun around, drew her weapon, and dropped to one knee. It sounded as if someone had entered through the door behind her. She remained silent, straining her eyes and her ears in the quiet darkness. Exhaling the breath she held in her lungs, she stood and slipped the derringer back into her right pocket, snapping on the flashlight, and turned back toward her destination.

Her heart pounded in her chest, now loud enough for her to hear. Taking another deep breath, she hesitated at the door leading into the hallway. The door's hinges groaned as she pushed it open using the toe of her right boot.

Sweeping the flashlight's beam down the hall, Fay counted three doors on the left wall, then tiptoed along the hallway to the third door and paused. "I'm at the door," she announced. "Are you alone?"

"I'm here," the man's hollow voice called from inside the room. "I'm alone. Come in."

Fay released her grip on the derringer, removed her right hand from her coat pocket, turned the knob, placed her right hand back into her pocket, and grasped the derringer. She pushed the door open with the flashlight in her left hand. "I'm not coming into a dark room," she said.

The man struck a match. A disembodied flame traveled a short distance through the air. Soon, the soft glow of an oil lamp lit the room in an eerie light, the yellow flickering flame now reflecting on the man's demonic face.

She entered the room. "A bit melodramatic, don't you think?"

"Fay, it's so nice to see you again."

"Cut the crap, you piece of shit. I agreed to meet you here. I didn't agree to be sociable."

"Fair enough," he said in a patient voice. "Come in." He rose from a hard-backed wooden chair placed next to the table. Pointing at a similar chair, he said, "Have a seat."

"I'll stand. Did you bring it?" Fay asked as she drew her derringer from her coat pocket, revealing it to him for the first time.

His gaze shifted, and he noticed the weapon. A slight smile formed on his lips, but he remained silent.

"This can be as quick and painless as you want it to be," Fay said. "Toss me the list, and I'm gone from your life."

He reached inside his jacket.

"Easy," she cautioned, pointing the derringer at him.

"No problem." He removed a small black notebook from his jacket and tossed it onto the table. Nodding in its direction, he said, "Transaction completed."

Fay stepped further into the room and kept her gaze trained on the man.

"What now?" he asked.

In dealing with snakes, know three things, Fay silently reminded herself: *they will eat anything smaller than they are, they are afraid of anything more significant than they are, and they will attack if threatened*. "You beat me and raped me, you poor excuse for an asshole," she accused.

"That was unfortunate," the man coolly replied.

"Unfortunate?" Fay paused, flashing an angry sneer at him. "What really pissed me off is you ruined my favorite dress. I'd waste you right here, right now, if I thought it would make a difference. But it wouldn't."

"You survived. I'm impressed."

"I survived you twice, the first time when you beat

me to within an inch of my life, the second when you left me to die in the desert," Fay retorted. "I figure you've got a fifty-fifty chance right now of surviving me just one time, you pathetic piece of shit."

"I love it when you talk dirty to me, bitch."

Fay grinned. "You know, Justine, I'm not such a bad person once you get to know me. In fact, I've been known, on occasion, to take an ice pick to my heart, chip off a little piece, and present it to someone. But I have to really, really like them before I'm willing to endure that sort of pain."

He, too, grinned. "In another place, another time, you and I would have made a dynamic duo, Fay."

"Hardly."

His gaze shifted away from her and seemed to refocus behind her. His slight constant smile grew. The flickering lamplight distorted his features, making him look even eviler.

Fay had seen the ploy a million times in Western movies – it was a trick to make your opponent think someone was behind you. You lost your concentration for an instant, and your opponent was on top of you. She felt the hairs rise on the back of her neck.

"You there, Shaman?" Fay called. She hoped so.

Justine's eyebrows arched. "You two know one another?" he asked.

"Don't you move another inch," she commanded.

"Am I to believe you would shoot me, Fay?" He moved several paces toward her.

"I'm warning you. And you stay put too, Shaman," she ordered as she lowered the aim of her derringer, pointing the muzzle at Justine's groin, "or I'll blow his goddamn nuts off."

"Kill her, Shaman." From behind Justine's back flashed the silver blade of a sword. He lunged at her.

Fay held her ground. "Guilty," she said. She squeezed the derringer's trigger, just as little Abigail Caitlin stepped from the shadows and into the path of the fatal bullet.

"NO!" Fay screamed. Three shots rang out with a deafening report. She felt a burning, sharp pain at her left side. Her vision blurred, and she sank to her knees.

Abigail simultaneously sank to her knees, a look of disbelief evident on her sweet child's face. "Why me?" Abby whispered.

For a few seconds, Fay and the girl held each other's gaze. Both fell forward. Fay lay motionless on the floor, watching as a pair of shoes approach from the shadows. "Shaman," she moaned. She heard a click, sounding something like the hammer of a cocking gun. Everything went black.

Chapter 6

Fay awoke with a start. Noting the time (03:35 A.M.), she snapped on the lamp placed on the nightstand to the left of her bed. As she sat up, she clutched the bed covers up and under her chin. Her body, warm from sleep, grew cold when her dilated pupils refocused on the man dressed in black who was sitting on a chair placed several feet to the left of her bed.

"Shaman!" Fay croaked and cleared her throat. "Long time no see, my dear assassin. Although I seem to have just met you in my dream."

A slight grin formed on the man's lips. He said nothing.

"You ever think to first warn me with a phone call, maybe send an e-mail or text…or ring a doorbell, Jon?"

"Not my style, Commander. Good to see you again."

"Jon, could I offer a cup of coffee?" Fay asked.

"Thank you. I don't drink the stuff. However, I can get you one, if you would like," the man replied.

A shocker. Jon knew how to make coffee? *This could be interesting.* "Okay, Jon," Fay said. "You may get me a cup of coffee." She realized she had just asked a confirmed assassin to make her a cup of coffee. *This is insane!* She added, "Jon, only coffee. No cream, sugar, or poison. Okay?"

"Okay, got it. Coffee black, no cream, sugar, or poison," Jon repeated. "I will be back."

"I am going to make myself presentable."

Several minutes passed. Fay donned a robe, washed her face, and brushed her teeth and hair. *What am I thinking? Making myself presentable for a hitman*?

Jon returned with her coffee. "While waiting for the coffee to cook," he said, "I noticed the little fish in the aquarium on the counter. What are they?"

"Those are my pets," Fay explained. "Joey and Garfield."

"Last time I visited, you had a cat. What happened?"

"I gave the pest to my boss. The fish are much less maintenance."

Jon laughed. He was a serious guy, being a former commando, assassin, and killer of men, and all. It seemed flat-out bizarre to Fay.

"It seems every time we meet, we are either meeting in my bedroom, you are shooting me, throwing me away in a desert, or we are rescuing damsels in distress somewhere in the Czech Republic." Fay paused. "Crap, Jon, we do lead one fricked-up life."

Jon smiled. "Yeah, you are a classic yourself, Faydra."

"Those were the good old days, right, Jon? So, what's on your mind? You're not back in the assassin game, are you?"

"You will be happy to know I'm now both gainfully and legally employed."

"No kidding, you're back on our side again? Did the SEALs coax you out of retirement?"

"Let's just say I do work for the government again," Jon replied.

"Christians In Action?"

"Something like it."

Jon Shaman, a muscular man of average height, belonged to a breed of men whose dark, mysterious eyes seemed to be always dilated. With his steadfast gaze and his square jaw held tight, he was a handsome man, and an assassin.

Fay smiled. "I saw you in the park the other day. You're here for a reason, Shaman."

"It has to do with your upcoming assignment," he confirmed.

"I recently discussed it with...." Fay slapped her right cheek with her right hand. "You know I spoke to President Ross! I guess it should not surprise me. For the past twenty years, my life has been public knowledge."

"Some people thought it would be better if you came to a complete and correct conclusion," Jon replied. "So, here I am."

"Oh! Thanks for your vote of confidence!" Fay sipped at the coffee. "Hey, Jon, this is good. I think you might have another career choice. A coffee shop? It's safe."

Jon smiled. "What I'm about to tell you is classified. The information you will learn cannot be used or divulged in your green table proceedings."

Fay nodded. "Understood."

"The U.S.S. *Deception Pass*, an N.S.A. Special Operations vessel," Jon revealed, "is the successful culmination of the Navy's experiment during World War Two, known as the Philadelphia Experiment."

"Jon, I do not think you slipped into my bedroom, under cover of darkness, to romance me or to tell me about a ship or an experiment I already knew about," Fay told him. "There is more. Isn't there?"

Jon gazed at Fay much like a brother would a sister.

"Sometimes, I think it a pity you were not born a man, Faydra."

"Why, Jon? You did not turn gay on me, did you?" Fay teased.

"No. Hardly. I do and will always prefer the ladies." He shrugged his shoulders. "I just don't have time for them."

"Perhaps one day you will settle down. I know you would make some woman a good husband. I would suppose she would have to be a spy and all. The two of you could raise a fine crop of little spooks," Fay said with a chuckle. "At least she would feel safe."

"I've already exceeded my life expectancy, Fay. I doubt I'll collect my 401K," Jon said. "And I don't see a home with the white picket fence anywhere in my future."

"Now that is a sad thought." She frowned. "Get out now, Jon, while you still can!" Fay advised. Killer for hire or not, she did have a fondness for Jon - in a motherly sort of way.

"There are times I wish I could," he said.

Fay readjusted her pillow. "I am sorry, you were going to tell me something I did not already know."

"Yes," Jon continued. "*Deception Pass* recently returned from a mission."

"Classified?"

"Yes, and the mission affects you, so I'm going to tell you about it."

"Me?" Fay questioned.

"A six-man op was assigned to extract a former American, an expatriate, from a Chinese prison," Jon divulged. "The team was made up of three Americans, two Russians, and me."

Fay commented, "This is sounding more bizarre and more familiar by the minute."

"Me, three Americans, and two Russians," Jon repeated.

"I got it, Jon," Fay replied. "Please, details."

"Give me an hour, and I'll guarantee you'll once again believe in Santa Claus."

"What, Jon? Santa's not real?" she teased.

"The op went as planned. A chopper flew us from the prison to the U.S.S. *Deception Pass*, then to a location in the Yellow Sea," Jon went on. "We were transported, or 'teleported' as they call it, aboard *Deception Pass* to a rendezvous with two Russian and two American ships located three hundred miles away."

"Whoa ho! Wait a minute, Jon. Give a girl a break!" Fay exclaimed. "You just downloaded a ton of crap on me. Let's begin with 'teleported' and who the hell the man is who you misappropriated!"

"Roman Justine," Jon revealed.

"WHAT? I killed him!" Fay burst out. "How...it can't be! I shot the low-life, pathetic, asshole son of a bitch bastard!"

"He survived, Faydra."

"Jon! No! Are you here to tell me I cannot even kill someone and make it stick? Shit, Jon," she cried. "Worse, he knows I am alive, and he wants to finish what he started."

"I'm certain it is his intention," Jon agreed.

"Your old boss. You had him in custody. Right?" Fay asked.

"We did."

"He escaped?" It sounded preposterous. "Jesus, Jon. I have so many questions," Fay said.

"Patience. I will explain."

"Aww….no," Fay wailed and slapped her right hand down on the bedcover. "He's going to cut off my head. Isn't he?"

"It would be his plan," Jon replied.

"Jon, why are we and the Russians concerned enough to take the trouble to spring Justine from a Chinese prison?" Fay asked.

"We spent too much time in Eastern Europe for you to not know why," Jon answered.

Fay ventured a guess. "Human trafficking."

"Justine has many oligarchs' favors to collect on," Jon confirmed. "Financial influence in Russia goes a long way with a government where corruption is not uncommon."

"True. There is a second more compelling reason, isn't there, Jon?" Fay guessed.

"It has to do with a joint venture, a Russian and American weapons development program Justine is scientifically responsible for," he responded.

"Justine is a genius. I will give him that. So, what is he doing?"

"The joint collaboration developed a weapon centered around the Karman Vortex."

"To what end, Jon?" Fay asked.

"A weapon able to emit infrasound. A low pitch sound not detected by the human ear."

"Okay. I kind of know what the vortex is. Humans subjected to the vortex become confused, experience nausea, their heart rate increases, and they experience a feeling of dread," Fay recounted.

"They end up going nuts," Jon added. "I would surmise the Chinese are unaware of the program. If

Justine had remained in prison much longer, there may have been a risk the Chinese would have found out."

"It makes sense," Fay decided. "So, what happened to him?"

"He and the team were taken to *Deception Pass.* When *Deception Pass* teleported to the rendezvous, it reappeared, but the crew were scrambled, similar to the Philadelphia Experiment. I think several of my team members' brains were melded with Justine's," Jon theorized.

"Not good. These men may have acquired the frontal cortex portion of Justine's brain, which is the area which inspires his murderous ways," Fay concluded.

Jon nodded. "It is a possibility."

"When these guys were debriefed, wouldn't the scramble have been detected?" Fay inquired.

"Perhaps."

"You sound hesitant, Jon," Fay said. "These guys were debriefed, weren't they?"

Shaman did not answer her.

Fay glanced away from him, "Holy shit," she whispered. Glancing back at him with a look of doubt in her expression, she asked, "I don't suppose we can subpoena you?"

A slight smile formed on his lips. "I don't exist, Commander."

"So, we're back to this? He is planning to have me killed again?!"

Shaman nodded yes.

"Will he ask you, Jon?" Fay wondered.

"Justine knows I'm out of the game. He'll hire someone else." Shaman shrugged. "If he were able to return to the U.S., he might do it himself."

"If not you, who will it be?" Fay asked.

"Justine seems to have found a home in Eastern Europe. If he's gone anywhere, he's gone to Moscow," Jon wagered. "If so, he would send a man known as Evilenko."

"Evilenko," Fay repeated.

Jon asked, "You know of Evilenko?"

"I have heard the name, but I did not know what it was."

Jon chuckled. "'It' would be a fair description of the man."

"It's beginning to sound like your guys lost Mr. Justine," Fay stated.

"Unfortunately, so," Jon confirmed.

"So, what is an Evilenko?"

"He is so-called because he is said to be a descendant of Andrei Chikatilo."

Fay said, "I don't know who Chikatilo is."

"Chikatilo held the distinction of being one of the most notorious serial killers," Jon explained.

"I thought that distinction went to the infamous Gary Ridgeway?"

"Ridgeway admitted to seventy-eight slayings. Chikatilo killed fifty-three people," Jon clarified.

"You said 'held,'" Fay responded. "Someone murdered more than forty-eight people?"

"A guy in Columbia who exceeded one hundred fifty," came the reply.

"That part sounds like Ridgeway. How do you know all of this stuff, Jon?" Fay asked.

Shaman shrugged his shoulders. "I don't know? Read about it on the Internet…I suppose?"

"Huh. You just don't seem to be the Internet type.

And this Evilenko is also a serial killer? Like father, like son?" Fay guessed.

"More like uncle, like nephew," Jon replied. "And no, he is not a serial killer."

"You sound like you know this maniac."

"Only by reputation. He's the best. Or the worst, depending on how you want to look at it."

"So, I need to get to Justine and finish what I started before he unleashes Evilenko on me," Fay speculated.

"Yes, you do." Jon glanced down and back. "I don't think with Evilenko it would be a quick kill and off with your head. If he has a chance, there will be a lot of torture involved as well."

"The Navy knows Justine intends to kill me, which is why I am now off the murder case and sent to the only place where Evilenko cannot get to me - an American warship," Fay stated.

Shaman affirmed her assumption with a nod.

"And you are here to warn me about Evilenko. You knew sooner or later he would find me," Fay concluded. "So, I'm your bait."

"True."

"Are you alone on this, or do you have help?"

"The Russians have sent one of their operators to assist," Jon divulged.

"Because he would know what this Evilenko looks like and is a Russian speaker?" Fay guessed.

"She," Jon corrected. "But yes."

"She wouldn't happen to be a tall woman, would she? Goes by the name of Irena?"

"Irishka is Irena Sergeevna of the Naval Intelligence branch of the Russian GNU, known as *Naval Spetsnazotvsi*."

"That's easy for you to say. I have already met the lovely Russki fem fatal Irishka," Fay said. "I suppose I should feel honored with two of the world's deadliest having my six?"

****

09:10 hours, J.A.G., Captain Vern Towsley's office

"I had a visitor this morning, Vern," Fay told her boss.

"Oh?"

"Jon Shaman came calling," Fay explained.

Vern asked, "Are you okay with it?"

Fay would have thought Vern would have at least been interested in her news. She sensed he knew what was going on. She continued, "I wanted to talk to you about something Jon told me."

"Regarding *Deception Pass*?" Her boss guessed.

He was in the know. She now felt comfortable to continue discussing her classified information with him. "I have an idea regarding the three murders, sir," Fay told Vern.

Towsley remained silent. He would have stopped her if he had sensed she was heading into the need-to-know territory. He did not.

"Sir, would it be possible for Petty Officer Winslow to pull the duty assignments for Petty Officer Caitlin and Sergeants Main and Adams?" Fay requested.

"I will have Don access it for you. Can he text you or call this afternoon?" Vern asked.

"I will be home packing for my assignment, sir. It would be okay," Fay said. "I am struggling with something. If my hunch is right, those men last served on *Deception Pass*. As crazy as it may seem, I think our three men came home with some of Justine in their heads. If so, I will have to determine how to inform Corry Markham. I think this information will assist him with his case."

"You are right. This is a delicate matter. Rest assured; I will handle it for you," Vern promised.

"Thank you, sir," Fay said. "I will leave it in your capable hands."

"If I do not connect with you before tomorrow, have a productive meeting," Vern told her. "I hope you enjoy the chopper ride."

He was right. She had forgotten the only means to get to a carrier at sea was via helicopter. If one had to fly, by helicopter was the worst way to do it.

Chapter 7

10:00 hours, the Ward Room, U.S.S. William Green, on station in the Western Mediterranean Sea (the testimony of the American captain)

Although the air conditioning system seemed to be working, the humidity and heat were not pairing well. Fay fanned her face with a legal pad. The inquiry had been underway for a long two hours. Much of the time had been spent discussing boilerplate matters and introducing the attendees. Fay stifled a yawn and continued to fan her face.

"These are the findings of the Mishap Board, dated September twenty," Cartright said, reading from a bound document which lay on the table before him. He glanced up, then returned his gaze to the record. "In the forenoon of Tuesday 04 March," he read, "the American destroyer U.S.S. *Vincent Davidson*, DDG-ninety-nine, headed north near the island of Cheju-do, in the Yellow Sea. They encountered a light wind from the northeast, and fog reduced the visibility to one hundred eighty-five meters." He stopped reading. Glancing toward Commander Rodney Wilson, the captain of the U.S.S. *Vincent Davidson*, he said, "Commander Wilson, will you tell us the sequence of events leading up to the *Vincent Davidson's* collision with the Russian destroyer *Vazhny*?" This was an order, not a question.

"Thank you, Admiral Cartright." Commander

Wilson took a quick sip of water from a glass placed on the table. "I had the watch," he recounted. "We plotted an approaching ship at a distance of three-point-one nautical miles on the radar. The approaching ship, which we presumed to be the Russian destroyer *Vazhny*, was heading south, on a near counter course with the *Davidson* and at a close passing distance. We hailed the *Vazhny* to establish her position and to confirm her captain had the watch and was aware of our course and presence."

"Was he aware?" Admiral Cartright asked.

"The Russian captain confirmed our echo, course, and speed, sir," Wilson replied.

"And at what time did the two ships collide?"

Wilson referred to his notes. "The collision occurred at eleven thirty-one hours, Admiral," he relayed.

"When the vessels collided, what was the angle?" the Admiral inquired.

"About thirty-five degrees, sir," Wilson said. "The *Davidson* struck the *Vazhny* just forward of the bridge."

"What was the damage to the two ships?" Fay asked.

"Slight bow damage to the *Davidson,* Commander Green. Just above the waterline."

"And the *Vazhny*?" she asked.

"A gash in her superstructure," Wilson said, "about fifteen feet above the waterline."

"Thank you, Commander," Fay said, making a note on her legal pad.

Admiral Cartright asked, "Following the collision, were both ships able to continue under their own power?"

"Yes," Captain Wilson replied. "We made way for Chinhae."

"Was there any loss of life?" Fay asked.

"One crewman aboard the Russian vessel."

Admiral Cartright stood. He moved to a plotting chart displayed on a wall monitor. "The captain aboard the U.S.S. *Gray*, three miles astern of the *Davidson* at the time of the collision, and the captain aboard the Russian cruiser *Moskva*, two miles astern of the *Vazhny*, have contributed information," he said. "The *Vazhny*'s courses and waypoints were pre-programmed in a DGPS (Differential Global Positioning System) of the make STN-ATLAS. I understand the system had been turned off."

"Correct, admiral," Korovin, the Russian admiral, replied. "Captain Rudin, like many Russian captains, does not use the DGPS."

Fay arched her eyebrows and set aside her make-shift fan. "Why?" she asked.

"It's matter of trust, Commander Green," Admiral Korovin said. "Often, these systems are found to be inaccurate."

"They are satellite positioning systems, Admiral Korovin," she countered.

Korovin shrugged his shoulders. "Many of our good captains are what you might call 'traditional' sailors," he explained. "They prefer the old ways."

Fay smiled.

Admiral Cartright returned to his seat and again began reading from a document. "According to reports from the site of the collision, the visibility was minimal, which is in the keeping of the weather conditions. Do you concur, Captain Wilson?" he asked the *Vincent Davidson's* captain.

"Yes, sir. For short periods the visibility may have

been as low as a few thousand yards."

Fay's cell phone vibrated. She thought about shutting the cell off. A message could be left. Yet, she was curious why her cell had service deep inside the hull of the *Green* to begin with. She glanced at the screen. It had to be urgent, and Jon never called. He only showed up unannounced in her bedroom when he felt the need to talk.

Fay spoke up. "Gentlemen, I have an urgent call. Can we take five?"

Admiral Cartright said, "Let's take five, everyone."

Fay said to JP, "It's Jon Shaman. Come with."

The two women rose and exited the room.

JP said, "What's up?"

"I don't know," Fay replied. "Jon has something he said I need to see."

"This is the same Jon who has little use for anything technology, unless it's spy stuff related?" JP asked.

The ladies found an out-of-the-way spot in the passageway.

Fay called Jon back. "Jon!" she said in greeting. "This is unusual for you! What's up, man?"

"Faydra, I want you to see this," he replied. A photo of the upper torso of a woman was then displayed on her cell screen.

It took several seconds for it to register in her mind. "Jon... it's me?" Fay guessed. "Well, it looks like me posing as Faye King. What is this?"

"A woman found dead yesterday in New York City."

"I was found dead in New York? I have to sit down, Jon." Fay handed her cell to her sister as she made her way to the nearby stairway.

Fay retrieved the cell from her sister, then asked, "Jon, do you suppose this is the body double who checked my sister and me out of the hotel in Phoenix while you and Stanton were busy dumping us in the desert?"

"I know it's her," he confirmed. "I met her at Justine's party."

"Evilenko found her in New York and killed her thinking she was me?" Fay speculated.

"Yes."

"Jon, she still has her head attached," Fay observed.

"I wondered about that. He must have realized the double was not you."

"It makes sense." Fay gazed at the photo. "Poor thing." Fay hesitated. "Listen, Jon, I have to get back to a meeting. Will you promise me, now I know you know how to use a cell, to call me later today?" she asked.

"I'll call you back later," Jon assured her.

As the two women walked along the passageway toward the meeting, Fay said to JP, "This means Evilenko is searching for me. But he thinks I look like my undercover other, Faye King."

"In a way, you are safe for the time being, Spider."

"This is good. Yes?" Fay wondered.

The meeting resumed.

"At eleven thirty-five hours, the *Davidson* hailed the Coast Guard and reported she had collided with an unknown vessel," Cartright reported. "The Coast Guard, realizing it to be a distress call, took charge, ordered a rescue action, and sent out a 'May Day Relay.' The U.S. Coast Guard vessel *Point Defiance*, along with Coast Guard aircraft and helicopters, responded. The first ship on the scene was U.S.S. *Martin Gray*." Admiral

Cartright stopped reading. Glancing toward the panel of officers, he asked, "Is this accurate for the record?"

U.S. Navy Rear Admiral Keller responded, "The statement is accurate, Admiral."

"So be it," Cartright replied and continued to read. "Captain Wilson stated he ordered the radar settings kept as set, and they remained so up until the collision. When you took the watch at eight hours, Commander Wilson, what was the visibility?"

"Three miles, sir."

"And the distance at the time of the collision, Mr. Wilson?" the Admiral asked.

"Visibility deteriorated, sir. I posted two look-outs, one on the port bridge wing, the other on the starboard bridge wing, as a result," the other man explained.

Fay scribbled a note on the legal pad. "And your course heading at the time, Captain Wilson?" she asked.

"I laid the course at three hundred-thirty degrees, Commander Green. I ordered our speed reduced to seventeen knots in the following current of three knots."

"When were you first aware of the *Vazhny*, Captain?" Captain Lavrov, the Russian Navy lawyer, asked.

"The radar man noticed an echo on his screen at ten degrees of the starboard at a distance of three miles," Wilson replied. "We plotted the echo on the radar and determined its heading to be one hundred sixty degrees at a speed of ten knots."

Admiral Cartright asked, "The two ships would pass starboard to starboard at a one-half mile. This is considered a safe passing distance?"

Fay scribbled a note on her legal pad and turned it to JP so her sister could read it: *Are you hungry?*

JP smiled and nodded.

"I was comfortable with the distance," Wilson continued, "so we no longer paid close attention to the *Vazhny*."

"Concerning the *Vazhny*," Admiral Cartwright asked, "what happened next, Captain?"

"Five minutes later, both I and the look-out on the starboard bridge wing sighted the *Vazhny*."

"And what was the *Vazhny* doing?"

"Making a starboard turn, sir," Wilson responded. "As the *Vazhny's* turn increased, I realized she would cross *Davidson's* course line."

"What was your order, Captain Wilson?"

Wilson reached for his water glass. He took a sip of water and replaced the glass on the table before him. "I ordered forward speed reduced to zero, and the rudder put hard to starboard." He sighed. "It was too little too late, I'm afraid. We hailed the Coast Guard on VHF Channel thirty-two after the collision. We stated the name of our vessel, what occurred, and that we needed assistance."

Fay jotted another note to her sister, adding at the end: *Remind me to not do this again!*

JP again smiled.

"Go on, Captain Wilson," Admiral Cartright said.

"Not knowing the extent of the damage to either vessel and sensing the *Vazhny* was be damaged worse than we appeared to be," Wilson continued, "as a precaution, I ordered inflatable life rafts manned. Two additional look-outs were posted on the bridge."

"Had the *Vazhny* given any acoustic signals for operating in reduced visibility?" Lavrov, the Russian lawyer, asked.

"We heard no signals, sir."

"Thank you, Captain Wilson," the Russian replied.

Fay wrote, *Lavrov is smart*.

"The result of the collision caused extensive damage to the *Vazhny*," Captain Wilson said. "One life lost."

"Regrettable, Captain," Russian Admiral Korovin said.

Fay could sense a hint of tension in the tone of his voice.

"The impact of the collision knocked a Russian sailor into the sea," Wilson said.

JP jotted a note on her pad, and the pushed it toward Fay.

Fay read the note and then asked out loud, "Did the collision result in a fuel spill?"

"No. The U.S.S. *Gray* followed U.S.S. *Davidson*," Captain Wilson responded. "The echo of the *Davidson* was visible on *Gray's* radar the entire time until the collision. The echo of the *Vazhny* was noticed by the captain of the U.S.S. *Gray*, as I understand it, but he did not plot her echo since the passing distance appeared adequate."

Fay stifled another yawn.

JP wrote Fay another note: *We are going to break in 10 minutes. You can make it!*

Fay spoke up. "As a precaution, Captain Bell of the *Gray* hailed Captain Wilson on the *Davidson* to advise him of the echo. Captain Wilson acknowledged his awareness of the *Vazhny*." Fay looked up and removed her reading glasses. "Admiral Cartright, will you tell me how the crew of the *Davidson* would determine the courses of the target echoes?" she requested.

"I will, Commander Green," he said. "But first,

ladies and gentlemen, it is time for a break."

It was the best news Fay had heard all day. And the day had just started.

****

The panel resumed.

Admiral Cartright cleared his throat. "The radar crosshairs are placed on the target echo," he said, now explaining how a crew would determine the courses of the target echoes, "and the 'target acquire' function is activated. An electronic cross marks the echo. Next, the 'target select' is activated. When the radar has made the necessary calculations, the result is presented on a menu on the radar screen simultaneously as a direction vector. This makes it possible to visually determine how different echoes move in relation to one's own ship, and it allows a rough estimate of how 'dangerous' an echo may be. It's also possible to detect any changes in the direction of the other echoes."

"What if one of these echoes is no longer of interest to our captain?" Fay asked. *My god, am I even interested in any of this?* she thought. *I think not. And yet, there is something here, yet unsaid, gnawing at my curiosity.*

"When an echo is no longer of interest and does not need to stay plotted, the crosshairs are placed on it, the 'cancel' key is pressed, and the radar function drops the echo and its up-dating mode," the Admiral replied.

"You are speaking of an American ship, sir," Fay said. "The same procedure would be followed onboard the Russian ship?"

"In this case, yes, it would, Commander Green," Lavrov answered.

"The captain of the *Davidson* plotted the echo," Fay said, "which turned out to be the *Vazhny*, at a distance of

3 miles. On the radar menu, he found the information regarding course, speed, and CPA he needed. This data did not trouble him, and he canceled the plotting to start plotting another vessel. A couple of minutes later, he repeated the procedure for the first echo and got the same data. After yet another few minutes, the *Vazhny* appeared out of the fog under a starboard turn on a crossing course, and thereafter, the collision occurred."

"Correct, Commander," Cartright said.

Fay jotted a note on her legal pad. "By using his radar in this manner, the captain of the *Davidson* deprived himself of the option of following an approaching echo's course and speed changes by means of watching the vector a plotted echo presents," she concluded. "According to the captain's statement, the radar will perform poorly or not at all at distances of less than one mile."

"The captain was asked if he realized it was possible to have maybe as many as twenty different echoes activated at the same time," Admiral Cartright said, "and why he canceled the 'old' echo before he plotted a new one. He replied he 'usually does it that way.'"

Fay smiled at the admiral and said, "Thank you, sir, for your detailed explanation. As a matter of procedure, I would imagine the radars in question were tested for accuracy and proper function?"

JP jotted a note to Fay: *Why so much discussion about echoes?*

Fay wrote back: *There is a ship not accounted for*.

Chapter 8

Fay was reviewing her notes for the day on her tablet when her cell chimed. The display indicated "UNKNOWN." She suspected it to be Jon.

She clicked the phone on. "Fay Green."

"Commander Green," a male voice responded.

"Dr. Carlin," she replied. It was Jon Shaman, aka Dr. Carlin.

"Evenin', ma'am," Jon replied. "I trust your day went well?"

"Boring."

"Sorry to hear."

She enjoyed her conversations with Jon. Despite his chosen profession as a hitman, assassin, and killer of men, his voice always had a soft, soothing, and reassuring tone. "What do you have for me, Doctor?" Fay asked.

"The woman I spoke to you about today."

"The other me found dead in New York this week," Fay acknowledged. "I feel very sad to be the cause of another woman's death. Has she been identified, Jon?"

"I would not hold yourself responsible for it," Jon assured her. "She was Bett Meris, an actor playing the part of Faye King. She did not know any more than that."

"Thank you, Jon," Fay said. "But why are you calling?"

"I am thinking about our next move," Jon

responded. "Evilenko knows he killed the wrong woman. He is a single-minded machine. He will continue searching for Faye King. My fear is, sooner or later, he, or Justine, may realize your Faye King is a ruse. Should he realize Faye King is, in fact, Fay Green, well, we would have a problem that could not be resolved."

"Justine has to be stopped," Fay insisted, "or I am dead."

"Yes. I fear it."

"Aww, Jon, you care," Fay replied. "I appreciate it."

"More than you know, Commander," he answered. "I, with your approval, want to inform Justine you were spotted in Eastern Europe. This will get Evilenko back to Eastern Europe in his search for you. Iriska can better manage him there."

"Sounds like a temporary fix?" Fay wagered.

"It is," Jon admitted. "Yet, this helps to better manage the situation."

Fay replied, "Thanks, Jon. Please take care. And, oh, should I need to contact you, do I still call the Fillmore and ask for Dr. Carlin?"

"That works." He disconnected.

Fay sat, thinking what her next move would be. She was safe from Evilenko and Justine as long as she remained aboard the *Green*. But she would have to return to JAG Corps in Bremerton, where she would be exposed once again. Yet, she reasoned she had lived eight years of her life with a Secret Service detail guarding her every move and nothing had ever happened to her. Jon, and Irishka, had her six. Besides, when push came to shove, Jon was better at protection than an entire team of SS people would be. She would be safe as long as her dear assassin remained safe.

****

21:45 hours

"*Da!*" was the reply she heard. "Ah! Commander Green!" Captain Lavrov greeted her.

"Captain, I'm sorry to bother you at this late hour," Fay responded. "May I have a word?"

"Of course!" Lavrov said as he opened the hatch wider. "Please come in!"

Fay smiled and held Lavrov's gaze as she passed by him and entered his cabin. A young man dressed in a black ball cap, blue jeans, a white tee-shirt, white socks, and sandals sprang from one of the two bunks occupying the room, which was heavy laden with cigarette smoke. Fay smiled at the man.

"Commander Green, my legal assistant, Lieutenant Nikolai Sorokin." Lavrov made the introductions.

Fay extended her right hand. "It's a pleasure to meet you, Lieutenant."

Sorokin shook her hand while he spoke in Russian to Lavrov.

Lavrov replied, speaking to Fay in English, "Nikolai asks if he should leave?"

"No, no," she said. "I'll only be a few minutes."

"Please, Commander, have a seat." Lavrov pointed toward a chair placed next to a small table set near the bulkhead.

Fay smiled and sat.

Lavrov sat across the table from her. "Can I offer you coffee?" he asked.

"No, thank you," she replied as she surveyed the surface of the table, her gaze settling on a half-full bottle of Russian vodka.

"Perhaps you would like wodka, Commander?"

Lavrov offered.

"Vodka would be perfect." Her face brightened. "Thank you, Captain."

He retrieved a clean, beige-colored coffee mug from a nearby shelf. He then poured several ounces of vodka into the mug before pouring an equal amount into the mugs she presumed the two Russians had been drinking from. Lavrov set the bottle down and handed her the mug.

Holding his mug aloft as to signal a toast, he said, as Fay and Sorokin too raised their mugs, "To your good fortune and health, Commander Green."

The three people clinked mugs. She watched as Lavrov and Sorokin downed their servings of vodka in one quick gulp. Lavrov nodded toward Fay and tipped his cup to his lips. She understood the meaning of his gesture and, after placing the mug to her lips, tilted her head back and downed her vodka in one swift gulp.

"Wodka is for drinking, Commander Green. Not for sipping like wine," Lavrov intoned.

Fay believed Russian vodka rated about 90% pure alcohol. Most bathroom disinfectants were not equal in strength to Russian vodka. Oh my, did it ever burn as Satan's brew traveled the distance from her throat to her stomach. *Yeow!* She must have made an awful face because both men laughed.

Captain Alexander Lavrov was an attractive man. He was not tall but was about her height, 5' 9", and fit; she estimated him to be about 50 years of age. Yet again, he could be older. He laughed again as he passed his hand over his short, grey flecked black hair that was brushed forward from his temples. Dark, emotion-filled eyes highlighted his handsome, rugged, and tanned face.

She thought it a pity he wore a gold wedding band on his left ring finger.

Lieutenant Nikolai Sorokin was a tall and thin man with sandy brown hair. He looked to be about 35 years of age. The gaze in his sky-blue eyes appeared to be distant; yet again, it might have been the vodka that set a subtle glaze upon them. Nikolai spoke some English but chose (whether from embarrassment or not, she could not tell) to speak Russian. Since her arrival, he had not taken his gaze from her.

Nikolai spoke to Lavrov again in Russian.

Alexander smiled and nodded in apparent agreement. "You are right, my friend," he responded. His gaze shifted to Fay. "Kloya says he thinks American women are very beautiful."

Fay felt a blush fill her cheeks. "Kloya, sir?" she asked, confused.

"Kloya is short version for Nikolai. Yet, I can't say I disagree with him, either," Lavrov said.

"Why… thank you both," she said and demurely lowered her eyelids. "Alexander, sir, is there such a name as Kloya for you as well?"

"Is Sasha." Lavrov held up his mug. "More wodka, Commander Green?" He asked in a spirited voice.

A challenge, perhaps? "Please," she replied. How could she refuse?

Sasha poured more rounds as Fay and Kloya held their mugs steady for him. He poured himself a round; he set the bottle down. Holding his mug aloft, he said, "a toast," and stood. "To all of the beautiful American women. Tonight, two humble Russian sailors have great pleasure to toast their queen."

My word! Left speechless, Fay lifted her mug,

smiled, and downed her dose of white lightning. *YEOW! It goes down much easier the second time, doesn't it?!*

"Another!" Sasha announced and proceeded to pour another round.

Fay watched as he filled each mug with more generous portions this time. "May I toast?" She asked the men.

"Please, Commander," Sasha said.

Fay rose from her chair. Holding her mug with her right arm outstretched toward the two Russian sailors, she said, "You boys should call me Fay. Yet, I want to toast my handsome Russian gentlemen, Kloya and Sasha. May your seas always be calm. May all of your trials be hard-fought and won. May you always know success, and may you have a love of family. May you always share good vodka with friends."

The two Russians stood. The three sailors touched their mugs together. "*Salute!*" Kloya and Sasha exclaimed. Each one drank down their vodka.

"Fay," Kloya asked in English as he placed his empty mug on the table, "is true ship bears family name?"

Fay sighed. "I'd almost forgotten. Yes. It's true."

Kloya seemed impressed.

"This ship bears my father's name," Fay explained, "William Green."

"He was your President. Yes?" Kloya asked. "Your father must have been great man to have such great ship bear his name."

A tear formed in the corner of each of her eyes. "Yeah…my father was a good guy, alright. Tell me of your family, Kloya," Fay said.

Kloya smiled. "I am divorced, Commander. I have daughter."

"How old is she?" Fay asked.

"She will be nine years come spring." He reached for a small black nylon bag. Removing a stack of photographs, held together by a rubber band, he offered them to Fay.

"Thank you," she said and smiled. After removing the rubber band and placing it on the table, she reviewed the photographs. Many were worn as if they had been viewed many times. And rightly so, as Khoya's daughter appeared happy and beautiful. Fay selected an interesting photo and held it for Kloya to see. "Who is the woman with your daughter?" she inquired.

"It is her mother," he said.

Fay studied the photograph. "Your wife is a beautiful woman. I'm sorry it did not work out for you. Your daughter is so sweet. What is her name?"

"Her name is Larisa. I call her Lara," Kloya replied.

"Oh! Yes! Lara. I know this name from my favorite motion picture, 'Doctor Zhivago,'" Fay exclaimed. "Do you know it?"

"Yes, Fay. Is Boris Pasternak's book same name. I have read this book." Kloya smiled. "In Russia, what have word 'faya.' It means sprite or pixie. I think this is you, Fay?"

Fay did not often find herself blushing. But this comment brought one on. "I would hope so, Kloya," she replied. "Thank you!"

Sasha spoke next. "Do you have children, Fay?"

"I do not. I do have a wonderful sister," she acknowledged. "Perhaps you have noticed her at the inquiry? The Petty Officer with the black hair?"

Kloya smiled. "This goddess! Yes! She is your family? As I said before, American women are very beautiful."

"My sister will be pleased to know it, Kloya. Thank you." Fay continued to view the photographs. "How long has it been since you last saw Lara?" she asked.

He considered her question. "Perhaps one year? Maybe fourteen months?"

"Why? I mean, you did not visit with her on your leave?"

"We both have not had leave for one year, Fay."

Fay looked toward Sasha with questioning eyes. "One year?"

He nodded yes. "Russian Navy is not American Navy, Fay. Sometimes service to country is more important than service to family."

"How about you, Sasha? When last did you see your family?" she inquired.

"Like Kloya said, maybe fourteen months. I have daughter," he said.

Fay held up her left hand, with the backside toward Sasha, and tapped her left ring finger with the tip of her right index finger. "You wear a wedding band, sir," she pointed out.

Sasha smiled. "Russians wear wedding band on ring finger of right hand, Fay. I'm no longer married."

"Divorced?"

Sasha nodded yes. "I had son in Russian army. Unfortunately, he died in war. I also have daughter."

"I'm sorry to hear it," Fay said.

"Her name is Katrinka," Sasha explained, speaking of his daughter. "She is student at university."

"Is Katrinka happy and beautiful?" Fay asked.

"She is my greatest joy. And you?"

"I, too, was married once," Fay admitted. "It seems like such a long time ago. It seems we three have something else in common. Tell me about Captain Rudin."

"Rudin is good man," Sasha replied. "His distinguished career spans thirty-five years."

"I would have read about it in his service record, had it not been written in Russian," Fay said.

"Yes, Fay. Rudin's record is unblemished. It is pity we are now so near the end."

"Retirement?"

"Yes," Sasha answered. "Captain Rudin is tired. After so many years at sea, I believe he now looks forward to his remaining years with family."

"How so?" Fay asked. "Rudin is still a young man."

"He is Russian man," Sasha explained. "We are reminded our life expectancy is just fifty-eight years. Rudin is now fifty-five years of age."

"You make it sound as if he will die in three years."

Sasha shrugged. "No one can predict death, Fay."

"True," she acknowledged. "When last did Captain Rudin take his leave?"

"He has been at sea for two years. In this time, his son also died a hero in conflict with Ukraine," Sasha responded. "He has not met his son's son, now only one-year-old."

Fay cast her gaze downward. "I feel bad for him. It seems I keep asking why. Why has he not gone home?"

"The needs of the service," Sasha answered. "The Russian Navy has great shortage of sea captains. Captain Rudin lost good Russian sailor on his watch. He may as well have lost a second son. With all things considered, it seems to me he has now lost his heart as well."

"I don't blame him," Fay said. "What will become of Captain Rudin?"

"If he is cleared in this incident, he will remain in command of his ship. Otherwise, he will return to his home in St. Petersburg in disgrace. Now, if given choice, I think he would choose disgrace just to be with family," Sasha speculated.

Fay's gaze settled on the almost empty bottle of vodka. Without a word spoken, she grasped her mug and slid it across the table toward Captain Lavrov. He stopped the mug's forward motion just as the mug reached the edge of the table. A slight grin formed on his lips. Sasha took the bottle of vodka in his left hand and poured. After setting the bottle down, he slid the mug back across the table to Fay.

"I know Rudin will survive this, Fay, because he is Russian!" Sasha said.

"Russian soul, Commander," Kloya said, "something you Americans know little about. I think it is tough to explain because Russian soul is bottomless and unpredictable. I can't tell you what we will do in different situations because it depends on many things. You are a clever woman; if you want to learn Russian, like Captain Rudin, I'm hoping you will like things you will see and hear." He went on. "Russian people are very friendly, have very deep soul, kind and loving heart, and they always can come to help you in different situations only because you need it. For Lavrov and I to be lawyer in Russia, it's very hard way, because there always you can encounter situation where you will be powerless to change something. It's hard feeling it. But it's only life with good and bad things, because I have a preference to live life with passion and enjoy life and enjoy doing simple things as much as I enjoy the finer things in life. And so it is with Captain Rudin."

"It is a pity, Kloya; we knew a time when I could feel this soul on the streets of Moscow," Sasha said, "when the air was filled with softness and tenderness. Now, I feel sadness in my heart for the old mother-country, for a once glorious *Rossiya*… and for her proud and distant past. Now, my friend, as you well know, *Moskva* has become Western in its ways. But the soul…the soul now remains buried deep within her." Sasha smiled; after removing a cigarette from his left shirt pocket, he lit it.

He threw his head back; he seemed to be studying the overhead. Sasha returned his gaze to Fay. "Do you know of film 'Moscow Does Not Believe in Tears,' Fay?" he asked.

"I'm sorry," she replied. "I do not."

"This film proved a huge hit in *Rossiya* when released," Sasha continued. "I went to the movie theater with my parents to see it. I loved it, as I do now. Did you know this film was first experimental movie made in Russia with long run and big budget? We didn't care much about politics; we cared about each other. And the way how we were living and surviving as very simple. We were helping each other. This is what the film shows at its best. Real life, real friends, real meaning of life in our hearts. This is what I miss so much from that time of my life, and this is what I am trying to find now, without much success. Just how Vladimir Visotskiy said: 'This is very hard to find a black cat in the dark room… especially if cat is not there.'"

Fay looked at Sasha. "Russian soul. Captain Rudin

must get home," she stated. Her smile had a hint of slyness. Fay raised her mug. "To Russian soul," she said.

The three toasted. Still, Fay could not help but notice Sasha and Kloya were smiling as well, as if the three had come to a silent understanding this night.

Chapter 9

07:15 hours, Mess Deck, U.S.S. William Green

"I love it! This never gets old, JP!" Fay exclaimed.

"What, ma'am? The food?" her sister asked.

"No, the camaraderie," Fay responded. "Being here with our crew."

"I know! And you are also so kind when one asks permission for a selfie."

"The Seaman just now was so shy and sweet when she asked us," Fay said.

"Thank you, ma'am. I think the kindness goes much farther than it shows," JP remarked. "It led, of course, to the group selfie. Did you notice even the cooks came out of the galley for it?"

"I did! I suppose it would mean something to me if I were serving on a ship bearing the name of one of the crew to have a selfie of them and me," Fay observed.

****

Court of Inquiry, day five, 14:00 hours, Ward Room, U.S.S. William Green, (the testimony of the Russian captain)

"Captain Rudin," Fay said to the *Vazhny's* captain, "you were on the bridge at the time of the collision. Is this correct, sir?"

"Correct, Commander," Rudin said in English. "Collision occurred on my watch."

"You were aware of the U.S.S. *Davidson* and of her

course and of her location?"

"Yes, Commander."

"When you began your starboard turn, was the *Davidson* visible to you?" Fay asked.

"I believed U.S.S. *Davidson* to be dead ahead," Rudin responded.

Captain Lavrov, the Russian Navy lawyer, asked, "Was your course change to starboard part of your course plan, Captain Rudin?"

"No," Rudin replied. "I only turned when it became evident we might collide with another ship."

"The *Davidson*?" Fay asked.

"No, Commander."

"Captain Rudin, *Davidson* was the only other ship in your immediate area," Fay pointed out.

"We spotted a third ship, Commander Green," Rudin revealed.

"The captain of the *Davidson* did not mention another ship, Captain. Admiral Cartright," Fay asked the American admiral, "did any of *Davidson's* crew mention sighting another ship or noticing an echo on their radar screen?"

Admiral Cartright referred to his notes. After searching, he looked up. "The radar man on the *Davidson* mentions a blip or a shadow," he divulged.

"A third ship, perhaps?" Fay asked.

"*Davidson's* crew believed they were dealing with a radar malfunction," Cartright stated. "They noted the blip. It appeared and disappeared so fast, they thought perhaps it was a radar shadow from the *Vazhny*."

"The American lookouts did not spot another ship in the fog?" Fay asked.

Admiral Cartright again referred to his notes. "The

look-out on the starboard bridge wing said she thought she saw a ship much smaller in size than the *Vazhny*," he reported. "It appeared and disappeared into the fog. She thought perhaps she has seen a shadow or reflection from the *Davidson*. Whatever it was, it was not there on second look."

Fay looked toward the captain of the *Vazhny*. "Captain, was the ship you and your crew spotted a large ship, one the size of the *Davidson*?" she asked.

"No, Commander," Rudin replied. "It was small ship. Smaller than *Davidson*."

"Admiral Cartright, were there any other ships in the area and unaccounted for?" Fay asked.

"No, Commander. All ships were accounted for."

"Captain Rudin," Fay asked, "what were the course and the heading of the ship you turned to avoid?"

"We could not determine her course," Rudin answered. "She was dead in the water."

"Dead?" Fay asked.

"Not moving, Commander."

"And this ship you turned to avoid showed as an echo on your radar?"

"Not knowing size or tonnage of *Davidson*, we, at first, believed it to be *Davidson*," Rudin said.

Fay played out the scenario leading up to the collision in her mind. She now recalled her earlier dream; she, too, had envisioned a third ship. "When you realized this was not the *Davidson*, what did you do?" she asked out loud.

"I assumed *Davidson* would change her course to starboard," Rudin replied. "When I realized it not to be the case, I increased my turn since it was too late to steady my course."

"It is my opinion this accident was a radar collision," Fay said to Admiral Cartright, "where one vessel, in reduced visibility, makes a judgment regarding the collision threat which is contrary to the other's. This was complicated by the *Vazhny's* presumption of a third, yet unidentified, ship lying derelict in its course." Fay looked at Lavrov. A slight smile was evident on his face. "Numerous testimonies corroborate the presence of an unknown third vessel," she went on. "A ghost ship, if you will."

"I would concur," Admiral Cartright said.

Fay said, "According to the captain of the *Davidson's* statement, on the day following the collision, the radar showed the CPA of the *Vazhny* to be a one-half mile to starboard. *Moskva*, now on the same course as the *Vazhny*, felt its own passing distance to *Davidson's* starboard would be close. *Moskva's* captain readied to turn to starboard to meet the *Davidson* port to port. *Moskva* judged the CPA to be point-four miles if the courses were maintained. Given the two entirely objective estimates, it is clear the passing distance between the *Davidson* and *Vazhny* would have been very close if the two ships maintained their courses." Fay went on. "Had the *Vazhny* not turned to starboard, there would not have been a collision. The fault would lay with the *Vazhny*, if not for the presence of the third and unidentified ship."

"Had *Vazhny* not turned to starboard, she would have collided with the third ship," Lavrov added.

"The third ship remains a mystery," Fay said. "We should not rule out some kind of technical malfunction onboard the *Vazhny*, which would cause her to make the starboard turn when the two ships were meeting each other."

Fay motioned to JP. "Petty Officer, will you bring to me the manual containing the International Regulations for Preventing Collisions at Sea?" she requested.

The room was silent while Petty Officer Fletcher retrieved the manual and approached the court. After placing it in front of Fay, she gave her sister a reassuring smile as if to convey, *You are doing great, sis. Hang in there, girl*.

"Thank you, Petty Officer," Fay replied. After slipping on her reading glasses, Fay opened the manual to the regulation Lavrov had recommended to her.

"Gentleman," Fay said, before beginning to read, "Regulation 7 (a) of the International Regulations for Preventing Collisions at Sea states, 'Every vessel shall use all available means appropriate to the prevailing circumstances and conditions to determine of risk of collision exist. If there is any doubt such risk shall be deemed to exist.'" Fay flipped the page. "Reg. 7 (b) says, 'Proper use shall be made of radar equipment if fitted and operational, including long-range scanning to obtain early warning of the risk of collision and radar plotting or equivalent systematic observation of detected objects.'"

Fay looked up at the assembled court, took a deep breath, exhaled, and said, "The captains of the *Davidson* and the *Vazhny* made optimal use of their radar equipment, as regulated by Reg. 7 (a) and 7 (b). In keeping with the spirit of the collision regulations, any action to avoid a collision shall be positive and made in ample time and with regard to good seamanship. To this regulation and considering the possibility of a third and unidentified vessel, Captain Rudin of the vessel *Vazhny* is in compliance," she concluded. "Lookouts were posted by both captains. Compliance to Reg. 5 of the COLREG has been satisfied. Both vessels were operating at a safe speed for the conditions, which satisfies Reg. 6." Fay laid down her pen, removed her reading glasses, and folded her hands in front of her.

"Thank you, Commander Green," Admiral Cartright said. "Captain Lavrov," he stated, addressing the Russian Navy lawyer, "do you concur with Commander Green?"

"I agree, Admiral," Lavrov replied. "Radar collisions have been a matter of reality ever since the inception of radar, no matter how sophisticated the systems have become. Therefore, it is imperative to remember a navigator on another bridge may come to a totally different conclusion than one's own, especially when passing at short CPA. Unfortunately, we lost one life. We are thankful no environmental damage due to fuel spillage occurred."

"Thank you, Captain Lavrov," Admiral Cartright said. He shifted his gaze back toward Fay. "Do you have a recommendation for this panel, Commander Green?" he asked her.

"Yes, sir," Fay said as she rose from her chair. Looking at the Russian Admiral, she said, "While I can find no fault either captain was negligent, I agree with this panel that to lose a single life, whether it be Russian or American, is regrettable. It is yet to be determined if a third ship may have been involved. Yet, we have found no reason to doubt Captain Rudin did order his course change to starboard to avoid colliding with the ghost ship." Fay cleared her throat; she had not spoken to Lavrov about what she was going to say next, yet she felt he would support her. She started to read from a sheet of paper she held in her hands. "It is the opinions of both Captain Lavrov and myself, while this panel may wish to find fault concerning one or both of these captains, Captain Rudin should be held accountable in some way. With all due respect to the Russian admiralty, we recommend Captain Rudin be returned to his home port in Russia to begin serving ninety days paid administrative leave of absence. After such time, he will be allowed to regain command of a surface vessel if he so chooses. In light of Captain Rudin's outstanding and untarnished service record, we recommend this incident should not be included therein." Fay smiled at the Russian admiral. "Respectfully submitted, Commander Faydra Green, U.S. Navy J.A.G. Corps. Thank you." She sat.

Other than the shuffling of papers and a random nervous cough or two, the room remained quiet.

Korovin, the Russian admiral, rose from his chair. His face stern, he addressed Captain Lavrov. "Do you have any final words, Captain?"

"No, sir."

He turned toward Admiral Cartright. "On behalf of both the Russian Navy and the people of Russia, I apologize for this unfortunate incident," Korovin intoned.

Admiral Korovin next turned to Captain Rudin. "I concur with the joint legal consul," he stated. "Captain Rudin, you are with this ordered to begin a one hundred eighty-day leave of command at full pay and rank. At such time, we will review." A slight smile formed on

Korovin's lips. He sat down.

"All having been satisfied here today, this inquiry is hereby adjourned," Admiral Cartright ordered.

Chapter 10

"Congratulations, Fayzie," JP said, "you were superb today."

"We were superb." Fay smiled. "Great job, sis!"

"Too bad Captain Rudin got relieved of duty for six months."

"No, darlin'," Fay corrected her sister, "it was the best outcome we could have hoped for."

"We?" JP repeated quizzically. "I would think otherwise."

Fay proceeded to tell her sister about her meeting the night before with Sasha and Kloya in Sasha's cabin. She told her about their discussion about the Russian soul, family, and the unfairly long Russian duty cycles.

JP's mood changed from sadness to happiness once she understood the gravity of the situation. "You drank a lot of vodkas, it sounds like," she remarked.

"More than I hope to ever drink again in one sitting," Fay acknowledged. "Except for tonight."

"How so?"

"In about an hour, we are going to have two guests," Fay explained, "Captain Lavrov and his assistant, Nikolai."

"The cute, taller-than-me Russian Lieutenant?" JP asked.

Fay pointed toward two bottles of vodka placed on

a nearby table. "We are going to learn more about the Russian soul, and we will honor our two Russian comrades. We are going to do our best to make them forget about their loneliness. You are going to like them. I even downloaded lively Russian music."

A broad smile formed on JP's lips. "Cool!" she exclaimed.

"And they all have the sweetest of names. Lavrov is Sasha, and Nikolai is Kloya," Fay said.

"You, my dear, are…?" JP asked.

"I suspect it is 'Faya,'" Fay replied. "It means sprite or pixie."

JP snickered. "That fits! No one is more mischievous than you, my dearest sister."

"This may well turn out to be just what the doctor ordered!"

"Not to change the subject," her sister broke in, "but I will anyway. Why did you suspect the third ship was the U.S.S. *Deception Pass*, ma'am?" JP asked.

"Have you heard of remote viewing?"

With a look of doubt evident on her face, JP said, "No."

Fay smiled. "Remote viewers can project their conscious observation to a distant location to see or sense what is there," she explained. "Remote viewing was used for intelligence gathering by the Russians in the nineteen sixties. We Americans rediscovered it around nineteen seventy. Now, most intelligence agencies are using it to glean data from other sources."

"Okay. Yeah. I've heard about it," JP responded.

"You recall the Philadelphia Experiment, don't you?"

Jay wrinkled her brow. "I think I do," she replied.

"The Navy transported a ship and her crew through space and time?"

Fay nodded. "Kind of like that. Allegedly, a U.S. Navy destroyer, the U.S.S. *Eldridge*, teleported from Philadelphia to Norfolk in an incident known as the Philadelphia Experiment."

"That's right! It seems like some kind of *Twilight Zone* thing or something. It did happen?" JP guessed.

"No one has been able to verify the authenticity of the experiment," Fay said. "The crew of the American merchant ship SS *Andrew Furuseth* claims they saw *Eldridge* materialize in Norfolk harbor. Later, the crew of the *Andrew Furuseth* recanted their story."

"And you speculate," Jay said, "*Deception Pass* could have been involved in a similar experiment when it disappeared, but the Navy somehow lost it?"

"*Deception Pass* is a spy ship. How convenient would it be to have a ship which can appear and disappear at will?" Fay sighed. She lowered the tone of her voice to a whisper. "Last week, I had a dream, or a vision, if you will. I did not understand at the time. Now, I realize I was on the bridge of the Russian ship with Captain Rudin. I saw the U.S.S. *Deception Pass*, just as Rudin described it during his testimony."

"Do you suppose you were selected for the green table because of your dream?" JP wondered.

"No, I am here to keep me out of harm's way," Fay replied. "Justine and his hitman cannot get to me here. Although, you may be on to something."

"How? I mean, how would anyone know of your dream?" JP asked. "Other than you?"

"I wondered about it myself," Fay replied. "I researched remote viewing. Like I said, the Russians discovered it about ten years before we did. It's my theory a Russian remote viewer on the *Vazhny* sensed my presence or somehow knew I viewed the accident. The Russian remote viewer told their people, and their people told our people, probably PsyOps."

"Geez! Kinda like the *X-Files*," JP exclaimed.

Fay asked, "Was not the premise of the television program based on remote viewing?"

"I guess?"

"I do know I have limited psychic powers," Fay acknowledged. "Do you recall the apparition I saw when I searched Paul Charma's base housing? Everyone, the Russians included, knew no one would believe Captain Rudin when he testified he had turned to avoid *Deception Pass,* which had teleported to that location – everyone except me. Because I was there in my dream. No one would believe me to be aboard the *Vazhny* either, except for our PsyOps people," she concluded.

The expression on JP's face changed to one of concern. "Have you been having dreams relating to your assault?" she asked her sister.

Fay sighed. "Yes. They are becoming more frequent."

"Well, Dr. Gelis did say it is a good sign. She said your subconscious memory will link to your conscious memory." JP smiled as she reached to grasp her sister's right hand. Squeezing Fay's hand, JP said, "This is a good thing, Spider."

Fay wrinkled her brow. "I suppose," she said in a distracted tone of voice. "Huh."

"What's that, ma'am?"

"Back to the collision. Consider this," Fay proposed.

"Two Russian warships, one American, are all traveling the same course. The two Russian ships' courses mirror those of the American ship."

"Much like cars traveling in opposite directions on the same highway," JP added.

"Precisely."

"Each driver is aware of the other's position, yet one driver turns in front of the other. Why?" JP asked.

"The mystery ship, sweetheart," Fay responded.

"Could have been a boat? It surfaces, then dives. It would appear to have disappeared."

"Captain Rudin," Fay said, "would know the difference between a boat and a ship. No, he saw a ship."

"*Deception Pass*," Jay lamented.

"If it were indeed *Deception Pass*, it would seem she chose that precise time to appear in the paths of the intersecting ships," Fay concluded. "Why?"

"A rendezvous, perhaps?" JP guessed.

"That's what I'm thinking," Fay said. "For whatever reason, the Americans and the Russians were scheduled to meet at that exact location. And so was *Deception Pass*."

"Do you have a hunch, Fayzie?"

The sisters heard a knock at their door.

****

07:35 hours, Bremerton, Washington, three weeks later

During her breakfast, her cell phone chimed. She answered the call. "Fay Green." A large smile formed on her lips while she listened to the caller's greeting. "Captain Lavrov!" she exclaimed. "What a welcomed and delightful surprise! *Kak dela*?" *("How are you?")*

Sasha laughed. "*Khorosho*, my dear Faya," he

replied. "And you?"

"*Luchshe vsekh*," she answered. *("Better than everyone")*. "Where are you calling me from?"

"Moscow."

"Moscow! How wonderful! I am so happy for you! And what about Kloya?"

"Kloya is home with family."

"Outstanding!" Fay glanced at her watch. "What time is it there?" she asked.

"Six thirty-five in evening."

"And the weather?"

"It is warm; Spring may have arrived early this year," Sasha speculated.

"Wow! Captain, is this a social call?" Fay inquired.

"Perhaps," the Russian acknowledged. "I called to tell you I have your pen. You left it the night you visited my quarters aboard *William Green*. Can I send it to you?"

"I am on my way to Moscow. I should be there in three days," Fay responded. "I will text you when I arrive."

"Excellent! Let's make arrangement to meet! Will you need hotel?" Sasha asked.

"Yes!" Fay said eagerly.

"I will make arrangements. Near Red Square," Sasha offered. "Is okay?"

"Perfect! Thank you," Fay replied. "So, you have the pen! I have been looking everywhere for it. Korean President Lee Ka-Eun gifted the pen to me. I want you to have it, my friend."

"*Spacibo!* Faya. This is most special!" he replied. "Has the Navy been keeping you busy?"

"Have they ever."

"Oh? Anything as interesting as ship collisions and disappearing ships?"

"Yes, as a matter of fact," Fay said. "I investigated three U.S. Marines for the deaths of each of their wives."

"Interesting. When did these deaths occur?" Sasha asked.

"I'd say about ten days after the *Davidson* collided with the *Vazhn*y," Fay answered. "Why?"

"I recall reading something…" Sasha's voice trailed off, before he then asked, "Can you wait a minute?"

"Of course. Take your time," Fay replied.

A minute passed, and then Sasha returned to the conversation. "It is as I suspected," he announced.

"Suspected what, Captain?"

"We had similar event occur here," the Russian revealed.

"Military men returning from duty accused of killing their wives?"

"Yes," Lavrov said. "Two Russian Navy special operations personnel returned home for duty. The next day, both of their wives were dead."

"And this occurred on or about the same time as our three deaths?" Fay queried.

"I read the deaths occurred within several days of the incident you mentioned."

"What about the men, Sasha?"

"Both men are awaiting trial," Lavrov reported. "They will serve ten years in military prison."

"Is this a coincidence?" Fay asked.

"I'd like to find out."

"As would I!" Fay replied. "Is any of your information classified?"

"Some, not all. I can email what I have. Will you do

the same? I would like to know how the women died, and if the women were bitten, by chance."

"Of course."

****

NCIS Field Office, Bremerton, Washington

NCIS Special Agent Corry Markham felt as though he had hit the cliché-ridden brick wall. He had reviewed the statements of the three Marines time and again. The coroners detailed the times and causes of the deaths, with the wild card being the unexplained bite marks on the victims' necks and breasts. Those would suggest one killer, not three. One of the three Marines could be the assailant.

Corry felt the reports of Navy psychiatrist Lt. Colonel Garcia held a clue to the mystery. He reviewed each report three times in detail. He found it most unusual Doctor Garcia's evaluations had been redacted. The redactions made it difficult for him to piece anything together. He decided to schedule an appointment to meet with Doctor Garcia.

Corry scheduled a meeting with Doctor Garcia for 11:00 hours that same day in Garcia's Bremerton Navy Hospital office. Corry arrived fifteen minutes early. He made use of his time reviewing his investigation notes. His cell chimed. He looked at the screen. He very much disliked falling into the scam-call trap. He did not recognize the number; he did know the 206 Seattle area code.

Corry Markham did not feel he had time for anyone's nonsense, but something told him he should take the call. He answered. He listened as the voice spoke. A smile formed on his lips. "Yes. Yes," he said. "Yes. I can. No, when should we meet? No, I do not have an agent. Okay, I will be there on Friday at nine. Who do I ask for? Okay, Coach. I will see you then. Oh, and what should I wear?" Corry clicked off this cell. *Damn!*

Corry glanced at his watch. He still had enough time to call his mama. "Mama," he said in greeting, after dialing her number. "I got a call from the Seahawks! Tell Papa they want to see me on Friday!" Corry listened, then replied, "I don't know, Mama. Someone told Coach Bryant he should take a look at me. I don't know who!"

Just then, Doctor Garcia invited Corry into his office and offered him a seat. "Would you prefer a coffee, Mr. Markham?" he asked.

"I would. Thank you, Doctor Garcia," Corry replied.

"You are here regarding the evaluations I submitted for the three Marines," Garcia broached.

"Yes, thank you."

Garcia had what Corry presumed to be the three files stacked on his deck near his right hand. "What questions does NCIA have for me today?" the doctor asked.

"Your evaluations have been redacted. Can you tell me who or why they were redacted?" Corry requested.

"I am allowed to tell you who redacted the files and why."

Corry sipped at the coffee while he waited for Doctor Garcia to organize his thoughts.

"Because it is believed I will be called as an expert witness during the pending court-martial of Sergeants Main, Adams, and Caitlin, information regarding their duty status is classified as a need to know," Garcia explained. "I documented my evaluations as I am required to do. The Marine Corps redacted the evaluations as a need-to-know status. This will prevent me from revealing sensitive information regarding the three men's mental stability."

"Doctor Garcia, if I were to ask you if the men's mental states were 'normal' on the night of their wives' deaths," Corry asked, "could you tell me?"

"I can say, yes."

"Thank you," Corry said. "Are these men capable of harming a loved one?"

"These men are different by nature than you or me because of what they are asked to do," Garcia replied. "They are capable of separating in their minds who to harm and who not to harm, just as you or I would. They would not harm a loved one any more than you or I would."

Corry picked up on the inflection in Doctor Garcia's voice. "You said 'normal,' Doctor," he stated. "The opposite of normal is abnormal. Hence, the need for the redactions."

"That is correct, Mr. Markham."

"What type of person would strangle or drown someone and bite them?" Corry wondered.

"My evaluations were not extensive enough for me to place a label on any of the three Marines," Garcia replied. "I can say it would take a violent person to commit the crimes we are dealing with. The men are commandos. Commandos are not violent people."

Corry took another sip of coffee. He now knew what he believed he needed to know. "I want to thank you for your time today, Doctor Garcia," he stated.

Corry stood and offered his hand to Garcia. They shook hands.

"Have a pleasant day," Corry said in farewell.

Chapter 11

On this late October night, the flight crew dimmed the cabin lights; eight miles beneath her, a million square miles of black Arctic wasteland whisked by. Fay yawned as she reclined the seat to its full limit and snuggled the red wool blanket, imprinted with the winged sickle and hammer logo, up and under her chin. The blanket had a sweet smell about it. *Verbena?* She lowered her eyelids, her ears sensing the soft droning howl created by the plane's twin engines as it sped its way through the night sky.

Air turbulence would jostle the big Russian airliner from time to time, making it difficult for her to feel comfortable in the wide business class seat. Captain Semyov's earlier announcement cautioned all passengers to remain seated and keep their seatbelts loosely fastened around their waists. At the same time, he and his able crew charted their way around the fierce storm he said lay ahead. Although an experienced air traveler, Fay noticed every bump, every thump. Yet, the cabin attendants seemed oblivious to it all as they went about their duties of smiling and catering to their passengers' every whim.

If she were a tourist, there would be much to see halfway around the world. Yet, her state of mind would not allow it. For more than fifteen years, Fay Green had been a woman who fatefully served her masters of war -

a woman whose resume included such prestigious titles as lawyer, former First Daughter, and soon… assassin. Roman Justine had attempted to kill her, and she had tried to kill him. Both attempts had failed, and now, the time had come for the final game, the "rubber match," as they said. One would live, and one would die.

Sensing the cabin attendant placing something on the armrest of her seat, Fay raised her eyelids. The two women's gazes briefly met.

The flight attendant smiled and said, "Is special Russian cognac."

"*Spacibo*," Faydra replied softly, returning the smile.

The cabin attendant acknowledged her with another gracious smile and departed to attend to, and perhaps soothe, the other passengers' nerves. Faydra reached for the glass. As she brought the delicate crystal class to her lips, she thought to herself, *Russian women are so feminine, so elegant.*

The flight attendant returned. "My name is Sveta," she told Fay. "I will be serving you this flight. Welcome aboard."

"Hello, Sveta. Nice to meet you," Fay replied. "I am Fay."

"Will you visit Moscow this trip?"

"Yes," Fay confirmed, "only Moscow."

"Is first trip?" the flight attendant asked.

"Yes?" Fay replied, a hint of a question in her voice.

"Be careful," Sveta warned. "Is most expensive city in Russia. You must shop at Red Square. Before we land, I will give you some names."

"You are so kind, Sveta. *Spacibo*."

"You speak my language, Fay?" Sveta wondered.

"Hello, goodbye, and thank you," Fay told her, "that is about it."

Sveta laughed. "When I first saw you, I thought you were Russian."

"My full name is Faydra. Most call me Fay," Fay explained. "I have a Russian friend who calls me 'Faya.'"

"Faya! I know it! You are Russian." Sveta looked up. "I got call," she said. "I have to go to work." Sveta placed an entire bottle of the cognac on Fay's tray table. "Is long flight, Faya. *Agrav* is five-year five stars. The best for you."

"S*pacibo*." Fay thanked her. "I am so honored to have met you, Sveta."

Fay's plan was simple, spawned from an old cliché. Kill or be killed. She would arrive in Moscow in eight hours with but a single purpose: killing a man. A man who was an expatriate and, at one time, one of the richest men in America. *God has many mercies*, Fay reminded herself. Yet, she reasoned, her crime and her disgrace would be much too great to allow her to return to her beloved home, much less entertain the notion of her ever entering heaven.

Faydra had been brooding over her decision to go ahead with her murderous scheme for weeks. In the end, she had realized this was the only way it could end. Fay did not fear death; only the evil aspect terrified her, and she felt compelled to eradicate it. Recalling where her nightmare had begun too many months ago, she placed the now empty glass on the armrest and poured another.

Soon, Fay lapsed into a fitful nap. Although she could not see him, she presumed Shaman was somewhere on the plane. She could sleep soundly. Her guardian angel, assassin, and dubious friend Jon Shaman had her six.

The Aeroflot airliner touched down at Moscow's Sheremetyevo International Airport on time at 12:05 hours. Although tired, Fay managed her way through baggage claims and Russian customs. A hat, sunglasses, and strategically arranged scarf ensured prying airport security cameras did not record her true appearance. Sasha had offered to meet her, but she did not want to involve him. She had declined; she would take a cab. Sasha had warned her the Russian mafia controlled the transportation services at all of the major airports. So, she needed to be cautious about scams and overcharging, even more so if the fraudsters suspected she was an American traveler. He had advised her to barter.

As predicted, a short, busy man approached her. "I have your transportation to city. Follow me," the man declared.

"Hold on, Sparky," Fay said. "What is the cost?"

"Only one twenty American." He glanced at her. "For you, only one hundred."

"*Spacibo*, I can find my own transportation," Fay told him.

"This is difficult time of day. You will have to leave property to find transportation," the man insisted.

Sasha had told her the mafia did not allow independent drivers access to the airport property.

"I can see what I can do. But it will take much time," the Russian man said. "Is eighty American okay?"

Thus far, she had bartered down from one-twenty American to eighty. "Okay, I can do that," Fay said.

They proceeded to the passenger loading area, where the man hailed the next cab. He asked her the name of her hotel.

"Ritz-Carlton, Moscow," she said.

When her luggage was loaded into the car, they sped away.

Twenty minutes into the ride, the driver slowed the car and pulled to the side of the freeway.

"Do we have a problem?" Fay asked.

"I need forty more American," he demanded.

Now, the fare had increased back to one-twenty American. Fay had no options. The pirate had stopped in the middle of nowhere. He had her between a rock and a hard place. Tired and out of patience, she reached into her pocketbook, drew her derringer, and planted it into the frightened driver's neck.

"Drive, Boris," Fay demanded.

The remainder of the ride from the airport to the hotel could well have been driven in a new world record.

When Fay arrived at the Ritz, she was thinking about the forty American. After all, it was the Russian mafia she had chosen to deal with. No telling if the poor sap would find his way onto someone's shit list. She gave the guy the forty, plus a ten dollar tip. She hoped he would be able to keep the ten and buy something for his family with it.

Fay proceeded to check in. Her room was smaller than a comparable American hotel room but was modern and clean. While changing out of her traveling clothes, she clicked on the TV. The program, with lots of brash music and animated Russian speaking, appeared to be a game show. Although she had no idea what they were trying to accomplish, there were a lot of gayeties to be had by all.

Fay clicked through several channels, only to find

something familiar to her: an American movie. The actors were speaking Russian with English subtitles. Fay watched for a minute. "No way," she said out loud. She recognized both the actors and the unmistakable scenery of Seattle. "What the hell…?" she said to herself. It was now-deceased actor Heath Ledger and Julia Stiles, staring in the iconic comedy classic *10 Things I Hate About You*. She had left Seattle, traveled halfway around the world, and was now back in Seattle again via the magic of television.

****

The following morning, Fay called Sasha. They agreed to meet for lunch at the Ritz around 1:00 P.M. She had not seen Jon Shaman and wondered what he might be up to. The odds were better than good he had his eye on her from afar. She wanted to shop. She could walk to one of the most excellent shopping malls in the world, Red Square, but dared not. How very frustrating! She ate her breakfast in her room and searched for another American movie subtitled classic to watch.

Near 1:00 P.M., Fay dressed in something warm and casual and proceeded to the lobby to meet Sasha. While she waited, a man approached her. He looked official, so he did not concern her.

"Miss Green?" he asked.

"Yes, I am she," Fay answered. Could he be the owner of the airport cab she had hired the previous day? Was this clown looking, perhaps, for more money?

The man had papers in his hand and an official-looking badge, but not a gun, which indicated he would not shoot her. His smile put her at ease.

He offered the badge. "I am Inspector Popov of Main Directorate of Internal Affairs of the City of

106

Moscow," he said. "Welcome to my city."

An official greeting party. How nice, she thought. Fay rose. "Inspector, how nice to meet you," she said aloud.

"If you are here for tourist, I am afraid weather will not favor you," Inspector Popov said. Small talk now aside, he cut to the chase. "A man known as Evilenko was murdered in a popular Arbat club yesterday evening." Popov studied her for an instant. "Woman matched your description. You would, perhaps, know of this matter?" he asked.

WHAT! She knew of Evilenko. *Popov is saying he is dead?* Out loud, Fay said, "I arrived in Moscow the day before yesterday."

"I am aware of that, Miss Green," the man replied. "We found a photograph in the man's pocket."

"Oh?" Fay asked. *Holy crap*! she thought.

Inspector Popov removed his left-hand glove, reached into his shirt pocket, and withdrew a small photograph. He looked at the photo and handed it to Fay.

Fay accepted the photograph from Popov, glanced at it, and handed the picture back to Popov without the slightest reaction. *Oh, no*, she thought.

"It is you, Miss Green," Popov said as he stuffed the photograph back into his shirt pocket. "You live in my city for less than forty-eight hours, Miss Green, and one man is now dead. Your passport, please." He extended his right hand toward Fay.

Fay retrieved her passport from her pocketbook and handed it to Popov.

Inspector Popov took the passport and said, "*Spacibo*." He examined each page of the passport and returned it to Fay. "You have traveled to many places in our world, Miss Green," he remarked.

"Yes, I have, Inspector," she confirmed.

"Is this your first visit to Russia?"

"As a matter of fact, it is," Fay replied. Popov was becoming way too nosy to suit her taste.

"And what is your business here?" the man asked.

"I want to visit Red Square."

"You are tourist, yes?"

"Yes," Fay replied.

"And you travel alone?"

"Yes," Fay replied. She did not wish to implicate either Jon Shaman or Captain Lavrov.

"When you visit Red Square, you will want to view dead Lenin," Popov informed her. "It is interesting how they keep body in good condition for hundreds of years."

Yeah, just what I want to see, another dead person, Fay silently reasoned.

Popov continued. "Largest bell in world and largest cannon in world. Anyway, I think you will enjoy it."

Big cannons, big bells. She wanted only to get the heck in and get the heck out. "I will be sure to include them in my visit," she told him. "Thank you, Inspector."

"*Paka paka*, Miss Green," he responded. "Have nice day."

Fay felt fortunate to rid herself of Popov before Sasha arrived. Ten minutes later, she spotted Sasha coming into the lobby. She stood and waved in his direction to gain his attention. And how could she have missed seeing him? He had chosen to wear what appeared to be the Russian parade dress uniform, complete with medals which went from here to there and back again adorning his chest. He must have come to meet her straight from work.

Sasha smiled and waved. He seemed pleased. "Faya! So good to meet you," he said.

The two people hugged. Fay said, "Sasha, my dear friend. Wonderful to see you!" She stood back to admire his uniform. "Sasha, you… you look so official!"

"Uniform is impressive," he acknowledged.

"You had me at *da*!" Fay said, in honor of the classic line from an old film.

Sasha handed her a small, gift-wrapped box.

Fay guessed it was perfume. "Thank you so much!" she said. "May I open?"

"Please do."

Fay unwrapped the small box. Yes, as she presumed, inside was a bottle of exquisite perfume. She read aloud the label on the bottle. "*Krasnaya Moskva*."

"This is Russian fragrance, although I am told it is most sought after by women in all of Eastern Europe." Sasha smiled. "It is you. *Krasnaya Moskva* meaning is 'Red Moscow.'"

After removing the bottle cap, Fay dabbed a portion of the perfume on her fingertip and applied it to the nape of her neck.

"Now," Sasha said, "men cannot resist you!"

Except for Popov, she thought. Fay smiled and again hugged Sasha. "Thank you so much," she told him. "I will treasure this special gift in remembrance of our friendship and my visit to Moscow." Fay stood back. "Should we eat here at the hotel?"

"Excellent!" Sasha replied.

Fay had noticed the Ritz-Carlton Lounge & Bar offered "signature afternoon tea ceremonies," although her curiosity favored the Russian "tea ceremony."

Sasha and Fay were seated in the lounge at a table

near a grand marble fireplace. The lounge itself reminded Fay of a posh gentlemen's club. It may have well been one during Soviet times. The room had the air of highbrow Russian. The setting hinted expensively, and she was buying. No argument allowed.

The waitperson delivered an English version of the menu and asked for their drink order.

Sasha offered, "Please, Faya, allow me to order for us a special Russian drink. I promise no wodka."

Fay smiled, and said, "Please."

Sasha spoke to the waitperson in English. "*Medovukha.*"

"Thank you." The waitperson smiled and departed to place the drink order.

Sasha must have sensed Fay's mind curiosity. "*Medovukha* is traditional made from honey, sugar, yeast, and water," he explained. "I am not sure how they will make it, but also *medovukha* will have orange, berries, and herbs. Is good!"

Fay surveyed the lounge. "How very elegant," she commented.

Sasha asked, "How was your flight?"

"Aeroflot is the airline to fly," she said. "The service is impeccable. I have said it before, the Russian women are so elegant. And the men are, for lack of a better word, dashing." Fay briefly reflected. "Except for the clown I met at the airport."

"What clown?" Sasha asked.

"The guy you warned me about. The mafia cab scam."

"What did you end up paying?" Sasha asked.

"In the end, one-twenty U.S.," Fay replied.

"It sounds rich, but I have heard worse."

"Yet, I feel somewhat dense having fallen for their scams," Fay complained. "Oh, well. I sometimes wonder if any of us have any intelligence."

"How do you mean, Faya?" Sasha inquired.

"Well, you know all of those huge radar dishes we have pointing at outer space, searching for intelligent life?" she responded.

"Yes, I know it," Sasha replied.

"Have you noticed not one of them is pointed at Earth?"

"Oh, Faya, you make the great joke! Yes?" He said with a laugh. "It is a good one. I will tell my daughter."

Fay had thought about what she would tell Sasha when he inevitably asked why she had come to Russia. How would you tell even your dearest friend you were in town to kill a man? Sasha was a bright man and a lawyer who could ferret the truth out if he suspected something odd seemed afoot. She did not want to lie to him, and she trusted him as well. She would craft a blend of the truth, while at the same time avoiding full disclosure.

The waitperson arrived with their drinks and lunch menus. Fay admired their drinks, served in tall glasses on a small silver platter, garnished with an orange slice and an assortment of berries. A sprig of herb was inserted in each pinkish-orange beverage. "How very nice, Sasha," Fay commented.

She removed her cell from her pocketbook, lined up the drink, and clicked a photo. "I will send this to my sister," Fay told him. "She will really like this."

"Speaking of intelligent life, I saw Inspector Popov outside," Sasha said. "Did he talk to you?"

"He did surprise me in the lobby a few minutes ago,"

111

Fay said. "A gruff little man."

"He is one to be wary of, going forward," Sasha warned.

Fay wondered why Sasha knew of Popov. In a city of millions, what were the odds? She thought it would be better if Sasha volunteered this information.

"You have not looked at your menu, Faya," Sasha observed.

"This is your home. You did a great job on the drink. Why not surprise me?" she asked.

Sasha smiled. He only glanced at the menu and placed it on the table.

The waitperson returned. Sasha said something in Russian. The man wrote it down, thanked Sasha, and left the table.

Fay fondly looked at Sasha. "What did we order?" she queried.

Sasha again picked up the menu and read aloud, "Burrata black focaccia, balsamic strawberries, grilled plum, and pesto." He looked very satisfied with himself. "And," he added, "are you ready for another *medovukha*, Faya?"

"Please!" She felt mildly overwhelmed. "And I had hoped to meet dead Lenin after lunch," she exclaimed. "Oh, well!"

Sasha laughed, then said, "Dead Lenin has been dead for one hundred years. I think he can wait for your visit for a few more days. The line is very long… but I know people who today will allow special backdoor viewing."

"Of course!"

"I make call," Sasha said. "We go after lunch." He removed his cell from his coat pocket and placed the call.

Animated Russian speaking and laughing ensued. Sasha clicked off his cell. "Okay, we go after lunch," he informed her. "We go see one-hundred-year-old dead guy."

"One hundred years! Wow!" Fay shook her head in mock disbelief. "And Tutankhamen thought he had it figured out." She wondered what Sasha had had to promise in exchange for a special preview of dead Lenin.

"After," Sasha said, "we visit Tomb of Unknown Soldier, a war memorial dedicated to Soviet soldiers killed during World War II. Changing of guards, you will want to make video. Is very ornate." Sasha's eyes diverted to focus behind Fay.

"What is it, Sasha?" she asked.

"Don't turn around," he warned. "There is a woman who has been watching us. She would be the twin you do not have."

Fay found it difficult to not turn around. It was not often one discovered another who resembled themselves.

Fay had a purpose: to kill someone, not to tour Moscow. Yet, she reasoned now Popov had all eyes on her, she should look like a tourist. It might serve to lessen his suspicions.

Fay handed Sasha a piece of paper. "The inspector's name is Popov," she said.

A frown formed on Sasha's brow as he studied the paper.

"You know this man?" Fay asked.

"I know of him," he responded.

"Will there be a problem?"

"There could be problem," Sasha explained. "It will depend much on Inspector Popov's political agenda. If he is member of the New Communist Party, our quest will be difficult one. I will have to do background check on this man. I should need help…and we will need a certain amount of money."

"You name it," Fay stated.

"I think nine hundred thousand rubles should do it," he said.

Fay did a quick mental calculation. "About twelve thousand U.S.?" she assessed.

Sasha seemed to appreciate the quick math and smiled. "Close enough," he said.

"Done! I will have the money sent to you via wire transfer today."

"We do have, how you Americans say, 'an ass in the hole?'" Sasha remarked.

Fay laughed. "We say 'ace in the hole.'"

"I said it right first time," Sasha insisted. "Captain Rudin's half-brother is President Rudkovsky."

"No way!" Fay exclaimed.

"Is way, Faya. Which is why Inspector Popov's political ties are of importance to us and our success," Sasha concluded.

"It seems like a lot to digest," Fay remarked.

Sasha offered, "Tell you what. Daughter Yekaterina is student at Moscow Engineering Physics Institute. I will ask her to meet you. She will help you understand our systems."

While they ate, Fay asked about the two soldiers who had been accused of killing their wives. "These men were aboard *Deception Pass*, weren't they?" she inquired.

"*Da*," Sasha confirmed. "I think you know we part of team your Marines were also a part of."

Fay had suspected Sasha was more than the Russian Navy lawyer he had first presented himself to be. "I think, Sasha, our meeting aboard the *William Green* was not a chance meeting," she told him.

"We were there to learn about *Deception Pass* teleporting capabilities and to protect our government's interest in her capabilities," Sasha replied.

"I agree," Fay said. She glanced at the lunch. "This grilled plum and strawberries, whatever it is, is marvelous. Good choice!"

Fay had traveled to Moscow for a sole purpose: to deal with Roman Justine. Although, according to Popov, someone had taken care of half of her problem, Evilenko. Popov had disclosed it had been a woman of her approximate stature.

****

Following the lunch, Fay and Sasha departed the hotel to take a short stroll to visit Mr. Lenin. The mile-long line appeared daunting. Those at the front of the line had inquisitive looks about them when the guy who looked like a general and a tall blonde lady walked to the line's head. Sasha spoke to the two Russian soldiers stationed at the entrance, who then allowed Fay and Sasha to pass through.

"Fascinating," was Fay's only comment. Lenin's corpse appeared as if he had died yesterday.

Following their visit with Lenin, they continued around the corner to the Tomb of the Unknown Soldier. Fay had not been prepared for the pomp and the circumstance of the ceremony. Fay could not believe how high the soldiers could elevate their legs, high stepping to what seemed like chin level as they marched to and from the post-change. They appeared much like toy wooden robot men, dressed in long black wool coats and the traditional grey Russian *Ushanka* hats.

Following the changing of the guards, Sasha walked Fay back to her hotel.

"While you are in Moscow," Sasha said, "be careful."

"I will. And thank you so much!" she responded.

"Tomorrow, you will meet Yekaterina?"

"Yes, of course," Fay agreed. "Text or call me with the where and when."

Chapter 12

She had a Russian sense of humor. "Faydra," Yekaterina told her, "you need me."

"How so?"

"You need to buy things. Yes?" Yekaterina pointed out.

"Yes," Fay acknowledged.

"American price here in Moscow for American to buy item is double what Russian pay for same item. I wait while you do math, Miss Green." Yekaterina added, "What did you pay for cab from airport to city?"

"One hundred twenty U.S."

"Holy Saint Andrew's mother!" Yekaterina exclaimed. "When you and I return to airport, we pay twenty U.S. for two."

"Ouch! You can call me Fay, sweetie," Fay offered.

Yekaterina smiled. "Okay, Sasha call me Katrinka, sometimes Kat. At special times, like my birthday, he calls me *Velikaia Knazhna*." She thought for an instant, then added, "My papa calls you Faya. Is okay?"

"Katrinka is a beautiful name," Fay remarked. "Do you prefer it or Kat?"

"Kat is easy to say. Is okay."

"What does *Velikaia Knazhna* mean?" Fay asked.

"It is silly name. It means 'Grand Princess' in Russian," Kat explained. "In English, it translates to 'Grand Duchess.'"

Fay remarked, "I can see it in you. It's not silly. My father called me 'Princess' sometimes."

They spent the afternoon working on Kat's English skills. It confused Kat how Fay said specific phrases. Looking at Kat's English study notes, Fay noticed apparently, Kat had learned British English.

Fay explained to Kat, "We Americans tend to restructure sentences, so participles are not used as much." She illustrated other idioms common to Americans, while trying to avoid slang as much as possible. Kat caught on fast.

Fay had been hesitant to visit the mall at Red Square, but Kat proved to be a good saleswoman. The mall located across the street from Kremlin had been converted from a multi-level Soviet-era administrative building. Fay found the temptation great to not buy a shopping cartload.

Fay wished she had more time to spend with her newfound friend. She promised if she would one day return to Moscow, she would meet Kat again.

****

On the roof of the building located across the street from the St. Regis Moscow Nikolskaya hotel, Jon Shaman and Faydra Green were waiting. They had been waiting off and on for two days for their prey to emerge from the hotel. A thermos of coffee and a flask of Russian vodka helped to keep them alert. The Mk21 sniper rifle trained on the hotel's main entrance had a single purpose: to kill a man.

Jon manned the binoculars, Fay the rifle. To deal with the boredom associated with the waiting, the two engaged in small talk. This was the last thing in the world Fay had ever wanted to do, but it was a "him or me" scenario. Jon was the expert, yet this was not his battle to fight. Today, he would be the teacher, she the pupil.

Jon was not the kind of guy one would ask about his mother and family. He was an assassin by trade. It made little difference who employed a terminator for hire.

Yet, Fay, being terminally inquisitive by nature, felt compelled to learn something about Jon. So, she asked, "Jon, you have to be the only person I will ever know who has been teleported. What is it like?"

Joh chuckled. "I knew sooner rather than later you were going to bring the subject up."

"Yeah, well, a girl has to know these things, you know."

"*Star Trek*. 'To boldly go where no man has gone before.' In a nutshell," Jon said and laughed.

It made Fay feel good when she could get Jon to let his guard down, even for a brief second. She reasoned it was therapeutic for him, anyway. "Jon, that's a transporter," she corrected him.

"I don't know anything about *Star Trek*," Jon admitted. "I don't watch TV."

"Not even when you were a kid?" Fay asked. "You were a child at one time in your life. Weren't you?"

"It does not seem like it. I was on my own since like five," he relayed.

"How is that even possible?" Fay gasped. "I'm astonished, Jon. Where were your parents?"

"I had a single mom. She went to work. I took care of myself."

Fay detected a hint of sadness in Jon's eyes.

He continued speaking. "It worked out for me."

"Is that even legal!?" Fay exclaimed. "Never mind, Jon. Forgive me. I am prying."

Fay thought it best to change the subject. "If we make it to the airport after this," she went on, "you, my friend, are going to sit with me on the return home. Besides, I feel I will need to protect you from those vivacious Russian flight attendants. And I have many questions."

"I was afraid of that," Jon replied. "I, like you, had some curiosity regarding teleporting, so I asked one of the techno-nerds on to explain it to me. Teleporting transforms an object into an energy pattern - dematerialization, she called it. Then, the object is beamed to the target location where it is reconverted back into matter."

"No sensation?" Fay wondered.

"It's instantaneous. Like a blink, and it's done," Jon said. "Some claim they experience a sensation similar to a hangover when the teleporting is complete."

"Hangover, you say? I must have done a lot of teleporting when in college," Fay said. "Is it something you sense is happening?"

"No sensation at all," he said. "The crew straps into seats, like one would buckle into a racing car, and a countdown begins. When we hear 'zero,' we are still sitting; nothing has changed. Although when we go on deck, everything is different. We may have left a sunny day and a calm sea only to arrive in a storm. No time has passed, but timepieces have to be reset." Shaman glanced at his watch. "Our window of opportunity closes in thirty minutes," he observed. "Otherwise, we are back here again tomorrow."

"Had I not heard it from you, Jon, I would almost not believe it," Fay remarked.

"It seems unbelievable unless you have experienced

it," Jon said. "The techno-geeks are an odd group, though."

"How so?" Fay inquired.

"When I spoke to them, they were knowledgeable about the process. Yet, they did not seem to have any personality beyond their technical knowledge."

Fay wondered, "Androids?"

"I suspect it," Jon confirmed. "I've interacted with the Japanese AI versions before. They are excellent productions, but not one hundred percent real. Although they are getting there."

At 6:43 P.M., just before sunset, Roman Justine emerged from the hotel.

"Justine," Jon whispered.

Fay had thought she had the mental preparedness for the task. But no matter how desperate her need, she was not an assassin. At last, the student deferred to the master. Fay handed the weapon to Jon. Yet, when the day was done, it was not who fired the shot but who paid for the bullet.

At 6:43 P.M., Roman Justine lay dead on Nikol'skaya Street 12.

****

21:00 Hours, Sheremetyevo International Airport (SVO), Russia

The boarding line moved slower than molasses. A man had died, and she was responsible, again! In another hour, with the grace of an on-time, she and Jon would be on their way home. The Air Serbia flight had a scheduled stop in Belgrade, then after on to JFK. She planned to spend a day in New York before traveling on to Seattle. One more hour, and Russia would be behind her.

Fay's imagination had her locked up in a gulag in

the remotest part of Siberia, should she be apprehended. Her luggage was securely checked, and her business class seat was assigned. Only fifty-five more minutes.

"Jon, I am going to the newsstand for magazines, gum, and a tranquilizer," Fay told him. Although the flight had been called, she estimated there would be enough time.

When Fay returned, she and Jon proceeded to the boarding gate. And there he was - the last person on earth she most did not want to see. Her heart, and her insincerity, were in her throat when she said, "Inspector Popov. How nice to see you!"

Jon must have spotted Popov because he vanished. And rightly so. He was more exposed than she. Yet, when push came to shove, Fay would take the fall for their escapade.

"Miss Green," Popov began, "as you can see, I have brought with me these men." He pointed toward two scary looking Russian men dressed in long, black leather coats

Popov had got the drop on her. The only remaining decision: to wet her pants now or wait until she found herself in the Russian court?

"What brings you here this evening, Inspector?" Fay asked.

"You know, Miss Green. It seems when you arrive in my city, people die," Popov replied. "When you leave, men also die." Popov was toying with her. "Why, Miss Green?" he asked rhetorically.

Time to rely on her years of lawyer training. It had worked for Bill and Hillary, often. Deny, deny, and claim a memory lapse. It was also helpful to forget everything. "Well," Fay said, "it is unfortunate, Inspector. I hope you catch someone someday."

"This evening, an American died," Popov stated.

"How unfortunate."

"We found a photograph in his room," Popov removed a photo from his jacket, handing it to Fay.

Fay accepted the photo and glanced at it. It was her, alright. By chance, she flipped the photo over. Shock overcame her. "Fay Green" was written on the back. Justine had figured her out. Had she not got him when she did, it would have been a short matter of time before his hitman would have found her.

"It is curious the man who had a photo of you was found dead in an Arbat club," Popov remarked. "Shot by a woman of your height and build. And now an American has a photo of a woman with your name written on the back."

"Curious, Inspector," Fay acknowledged. "Yet, I know nothing about it."

"You did know either man?"

"No."

"I had come here this evening to arrest you for one or perhaps both of these murders," Popov informed her.

"Oh?"

"But an interesting thing occurred," Popov went on. "My supervisor called me while I was driving to airport. He told me to turn around and go home. It seems you have diplomatic immunity. As result, I must allow you to leave my country."

This was news to Fay. She had diplomatic immunity? "Unfortunate," she said. "Well," Fay extended her hand to Popov and told him, "my flight is boarding. See ya!"

Popov paused. "Oh, by the way," he said. "Do you

know a man named Jon Shaman? We would like to talk to him."

"Mother! Mother!" a voice called from behind her. Fay turned.

Kat rushed up and said, "Mother! I thought I would miss you! You forgot your ring." Kat handed Fay a beautiful and expensive diamond ring.

Fay hugged Kat. "Thank you, sweetheart," she told her. "You did not have to come all of this way!"

"Yes, I did, Mama," Kat responded. "It is most important. You need me."

Popov had the most curious look on his face. "Is your daughter?" he asked Fay.

"Yes, this is my sweet baby girl, Katrinka!" Fay replied.

Kat said to Popov, "I spent entire day with my Mama. I needed to see her one more time." She then spoke to Popov in Russian. By the tone in her voice, it sounded like she was scolding him.

Popov shrugged his shoulder and said, "Good evening, ladies. Have pleasant flight, Fay Green." He turned and walked away.

Kat watched and then commented to Fay, "All dishes point to sky… searching for intelligent life in outer space. None point here."

Fay wished Kat farewell; as Fay spoke to Kat, she glanced over the other woman's shoulder. There in the distance, she spotted Sasha. He smiled and waved, then turned and walked away.

Fay hugged Kat. "Please," she told the other woman, "give your father a message, 'To Russia with love.'"

"James Bond!" Kat exclaimed. "I will tell him!"

Air Serbia Flight 155 departed Moscow on time. Fay

watched as the ground below grew smaller and smaller. She turned to her seatmate and asked, "Where did you go, Jon?"

"I spotted Popov," Jon answered. "Knowing we could not be connected, I vanished. I met a pilot who agreed to loan me his uniform. I boarded as a deadhead flight crew member."

Fay laughed. "Jon! What about the pilot from whom you borrowed the ID and uniform?"

Jon glanced at his wristwatch. "In a few minutes, he will come to in the restroom I left him in, in his underwear, wondering what happened."

The flight attendant served them liquor and took their dinner order. After she had moved on to the next passenger, Fay said, "All along, I seem to be a step behind from start to finish."

Fay reflected briefly. "Katrinka lit into Popov like one of the banshees from hell," she recalled.

"Katrinka can read a man better than you or I can read a book," Jon said. "She wanted Popov to notice her in a grand way."

"I'm having a blonde moment, Jon," Fay replied. "Help me out."

"Katrinka resembles you in a lot of ways. In a mother-daughter sort of way," Jon pointed out. "If Popov noticed her, he would realize she too fit the description of the woman who popped Evilenko. She became another name on Popov's list of suspects."

"She threw herself under the bus for me," Fay realized. "Jon, I feel terrible."

"Don't worry about Katrinka," Jon assured Fay. "Popov will eventually learn she is state property. He can't touch her."

"You know who Lavrov is, don't you?" Fay asked him.

"Lavrov was our ace in the hole."

"I am not surprised," Fay responded. "How so?

"Lavrov is as well connected with the Kremlin as you are with the White House," Jon explained. "He was always our plan B."

"And Kat? Not his daughter?"

"Well, Fay, would it be a good mystery if you knew all of the answers?" Jon smiled and sipped on his cognac.

Fay punched Jon in the arm. "Thanks!" She asked, "Will we be okay when the pilot who you borrowed the uniform from reports it?"

"We will be okay."

Chapter 13

08:30 Hours, one week later, JAG Corps, Bremerton, Washington

"Good morning, ma'am," Petty Officer First Class Winslow greeted Fay as she entered the door to her office. "Coffee, ma'am?"

"Always," Fay responded. "And good morning to you as well."

"Corry Markham from NCIS has called for you several times," JP informed her sister. "He would like you to call him ASAP."

Fay retreated to her office. She called Corry Markham. "Hello, Corry!" she said in greeting. "How have you been? Faydra Green calling!"

"Ah, good morning, Commander," Corry replied. "Good to hear from you. Thank you for calling."

"How did your investigation play out, and what can I do for NCIS?" Fay asked.

"I wanted to give you a heads-up formal requests are on their way to you regarding my investigation," Corry informed her. "The three servicemen in question have each formally requested you as their legal representation."

"Sounds like a handful," Fay commented. "I will look forward to the requests. You can assure them I will be honored to represent them at courts-martial proceedings."

"Thank you, Commander Green, I will inform the men, and if you allow, I will schedule a preliminary meeting," Corry replied. "What works for your schedule?"

"I will have one of my Legalmen set it up with you."

"Sounds good! The men were hoping you would agree. There has been so much sorrow and stress with them of late. This will serve as good news for them."

"That's great to hear," Fay said. "I will clear my schedule with Captain Towsley and begin my planning."

****

Pre-court-martial meeting

"I choose the number of jurors to be between five and twelve," Fay said to the three Marines seated at the JAG Corps conference room conference table. In addition to the three Marines, the room also contained Fay's competent Legalmen, Petty Officer First Class Don Winslow and Petty Office First Class J. Fletcher. "So, we keep it contained. I go with five."

All nodded in agreement.

"Now, no one here gives a crap," Fay said, "where I attended law school. You can bet your three asses one of them will be a Longhorn, even if they got their degree in basket weaving. And no one cares where I grew up; you can bet your asses again one of them will be a Floridian. I am going for as many Republicans as I can find. If they are old enough, they voted for my dad. And, lads," she went on, "this is what is known as stacking the deck."

JP spoke, "The JAG has opted not to have a prosecutor. It is going to make it much easier to control the flow of the proceeding. In the end, those five jurors will decide your fates."

Fay surveyed the three men. "What questions do you

have for me?" she asked them.

"Ma'am, what can we talk about, and what can't we talk about?" one questioned.

"When you testify, I will be asking the questions," Fay told them. "However, the judge may also ask you a question. Be truthful. There is no reason to say any different. But you should know the public and the media have a right to attend the court-martial preceding. You all are aware much of your mission is classified top-secret. You have to be mindful of what you say. Do not go into detail. Try to stick to yes and no responses. And to keep it less complicated, I want you to address everyone as 'sir.' Got it?"

Fay looked at Don. "Mr. Winslow, what can you tell us about the judge?" she asked.

"Admiral Brandon May will be the judge," Winslow informed the group. "He is not a scary guy. Admiral May is the CO for WARCOM, your boss. He will be sympathetic. Even so, this is not the proverbial walk in the park, guys. Be mindful of the jury."

Fay smiled at Winslow. "Mr. Winslow, I trust we have the combat fitness reports and the psych evals here?" she inquired.

"Aye, sir," he acknowledged. "I reviewed them. The fitness, in my opinion, is fine. You will want to read the psych evals, of course."

"I can trust there will be no surprises with the combat fitness?" Fay asked.

"Good as gold, sir," Winslow reported.

Fay estimated the stack of files placed in front of her. "Okay, lads, now tell me something I do not know," she requested. "Like why did you join, and how did you get to where we are today? Oh, and this could take all day, so give it to me in a hundred words. Mr. Adams…go."

Sergeant Adams cleared his throat. "After high school," he began, "I enlisted. They selected me for infantry, but I knew I wanted Special Forces. So, I put my time in and accepted. I have been 1st Special Forces Operational Detachment-Delta (1st SFOD-D) for the past three years plus."

"Good job, Sergeant Adams, but you owe me about forty more words," Fay told him.

Adams smiled. "Gee, okay. I plan on retiring from the Marines and one day hope to…." Adams stopped speaking.

Fay knew he had been going to mention raising a family. "Good enough, Julio," she said. "You are off the hook." She turned to David Caitlin. "David, you are up!"

"Well, sir," Caitlin said, "I, like Sergeant Adams, joined right after high school. It seemed the right thing to do. I planned to do four years, learn a skill, and use the GI Bill for college. That did not work out because I met Adams and he talked me into trying for First Delta Detachment. We both got lucky, I think."

Fay continued to look at Adams without speaking.

"I guess I owe you more words?" he guessed.

"Around thirty," Fay advised. "Guys, there is a reason for this. So, humor me for now."

Adams smiled.

From the onset of Fay's twenty-question game, Jody Main had been writing fast and furiously.

Fay smiled at this enthusiasm. "Jody, give it up!"

Jody rubbed at his forehead. "I graduated from Sam Houston High School in Fort Worth, Texas," he said. "I did not know what I wanted to do, so I went on to Austin

Community College. After two years at Austin Community College, I went to work for my dad. But it was a dead-end job. My dad served as a Marine, so he encouraged me to join up. I joined the United States Marines as a medic. Later, I decided I wanted Special Forces. I met Julio and David when they assigned me to their squad." Jody added, "That's very close to one hundred, sir."

"It is, and good job, Marine!" Fay smiled. "What we are going to learn to do when asked a question is to respond in as few words as possible." Fay glanced around the table. "Follow me?" she asked.

All nodded in agreement.

"I will be asking most of the questions, I hope. They will be closed-ended questions. Yes or no," Fay told them.

Jody asked, "Sir, what if someone asks for details?"

"Your go-to answer is, 'Sir, with all due respect, I do not recall.' Or 'I am sorry, sir. That is classified,'" Fay instructed. "If you think you are getting into a jam, look at me and say, 'Commander Green?' and I will bail you out."

Winslow offered, "If you are approached by the media, you reply, 'no comment.'"

JP asked, "Julio, what was your last duty assignment?"

"I am sorry," Julio replied. "That is classified, sir."

JP asked, "David, where were you on July twelfth?"

"I am sorry, sir. I do not recall," he answered.

JP asked, "Sergeant Main, are you a member of First Delta Detachment?"

"Yes, sir," Jody replied.

Fay smiled. "Let's take a lunch break," she

suggested. As all rose from the table, Fay added, "When we break during for court-martial for lunch or otherwise and should the media ask us a question, what do we say?"

All, in unison, replied, "I am sorry, sir. No comment."

Fay looked at Winslow. "Don, order in," she told him. "Nothing for me. I have an afternoon meeting with the base commander, Wallace, as you all know, and my boss, Vern Towsley. We are going to talk about you guys. So, all is good!"

"Aye, ma'am," Winslow replied. "I'll go to the Jersey Mike's nearby."

"Hey, tell you what," Fay said. Reaching into her pocketbook, she retrieved her car keys and a credit card and placed them on the conference table. "Take my car, Don," she offered. "When you are finished, I want you and Mrs. Fletcher to review court-martial etiquette." Fay smiled. "If I don't return before y'all are done, have a great day! And remember, we got this!"

"Sir," David said, "the guys and I want to thank you for agreeing to represent us."

Fay said, "It's the least I can do. I want to thank each of you for your service." Fay smiled. "I'm sorry I have had to confine you to quarters, but because we are involved in a classified top-secret agenda, we cannot risk exposure."

"Thank you, sir," Jody said. "We are staying in officers' housing. It is sweet! We even have special dining hours at the officers' mess."

"Well, you guys deserve the best we have to offer," Fay responded. "Enjoy!"

Fay retrieved her pocketbook and briefcase and left the room.

As Fay transited from the JAG conference room en route to Admiral Wallace's office, she passed by her office. Through the window, she saw something that gave her pause: a large bouquet of sterling silver roses. She noticed a card. She diverted her path to JP's desk. Her fingers trembled as she opened the envelope. The card read: *Enjoy your day! Love, Carson James*. Carson had not forgotten.

****

13:45 hours, JAG conference room

When lunch had been consumed, Fay's charges went back at it.

Winslow began. "Mrs. Fletcher and I are going to run down the court-martial process for you." Winslow looked at each Marine. "Take notes, guys," he instructed.

He waited while the men organized themselves.

Winslow began, "Commander Green will prepare evidence and consider witnesses and will file pretrial motions. There will not be a prosecutor, so Commander Green is obligated to arrange for all witnesses. We expect at least one expert witness. It may be one or more of the doctors who evaluated you. And expect the NCIS investigator to speak as well. You all know him: Corry Markham."

"Will the witnesses ask us questions?" Julio asked.

JP replied, "No. They will only give testimony. The judge may ask questions, but not of you."

Winslow continued. "Your trials will be before a five-member jury. They are called 'court members.' There will be a foreman, known as a 'president.'"

The men were taking notes.

Julio asked, "Will the court members ask us any questions?"

"They are allowed to," JP replied. "So, be on your toes regardin' y'all's answers. If you need a minute to think before you respond, do. It's better than blurtin' somethin' out."

Winslow resumed speaking. "Commander Green will choose the court members. The Commander will know or will interview them before she selects them."

"Excuse me, Mr. Winslow," Jody said. "This might get confusing. Would it be a good idea for us to have a spokesman?"

Winslow's eyes lit up. "I think so, Jody," he replied. "It would help us to keep our events straight. Who would it be?"

"I think we would volunteer David, sir," Jody said.

"Gee, thanks," David said. "I will do it!"

"Cool!" Winslow said. "Was he your team leader on your last op?"

Jody hesitated and then replied, "I don't recall, sir."

Both Winslow and JP laughed and clapped.

"Perfect, Jody!" JP exclaimed. "But he almost had you, I think?"

"Well done, Jody," Winslow added.

A voice from the conference room door said, "I heard that!" It was Fay. "Well done, Mr. Main," she said. "I overheard y'all from outside. From what I have heard, y'all are on point! Carry on, guys. I just stopped in to get a file."

Fay retrieved the file and left the room.

Winslow continued. "The panel members will be questioned by Commander Green. This questioning is called *voir dire*. In other words, will they be fair and impartial? We need to assure the potential jurors know you are innocent until proven guilty."

JP continued, "The members of the court members have to be your rank or above. Because you are enlisted service members, you can request at least one-third of the jury be of your same rank." JP looked at the three men. "So, what do y'all think, guys?" she asked.

The Marines discussed their options. When it appeared they had come to an agreement, David replied, "We want to go any equal rank or higher."

Winslow jotted a note. "Okay." He glanced up at Julio. "Julio, you don't look well, man," he observed. "Are you okay?"

Julio was white and appeared to be perspiring. "I'm okay."

Winslow knew the Marine in him was talking, and that Julio was not actually okay. "Let's get him a glass of water and get him over to the couch over there," Winslow ordered.

JP had a concerned look on her face. "I'm gonna call Sickbay. Have them make a hole for us," she said. "I'll run and get a cold towel for his forehead."

When JP returned with the towel, Julio laid down on the couch. Still, his condition did not appear to improve.

"Don, I don't think Julio should be moved," JP said. "Will you call a corpsman in an emergency?"

"Do we want to text Commander Green?" Winslow asked.

"Let's wait to find out what we have first," JP replied.

****

Thirty minutes later

Two Navy corpsmen arrived at the JAG conference room. Corpsmen Johanson and Vega-Martinez attended to Julio with urgency.

135

"You are going to be okay, Sergeant," Vega-Martinez said. "Show me what you are feeling."

Julio winced, pointing to his right abdomen area.

"Julio, we are going to take you to the hospital," Vega-Martinez said. She patted him on the shoulder. "You are going to be okay." She looked in the direction of the others in the room. "Will one of you meet us at the hospital?" she requested.

Winslow looked at JP. She nodded. "We will all meet you there," she answered.

The corpsmen rushed Julio from the conference room to a waiting ambulance.

****

21:10 Hours, Navy Hospital, Bremerton

Fay, Don, JP, Jody, and David were waiting with anticipation in the Navy hospital surgery recovery's lobby for the first word about Julio's emergency laparoscopic surgery. In the more than one hour Fay had been staying there, she had consumed three cups of her beverage of choice: strong, black coffee. Any brand would do.

Fifteen minutes later, an orderly entered the lobby, asking for Commander Green and her party.

"That's me!" Fay exclaimed.

The orderly made her way to Fay and her group. "Sergeant Adams' laparoscopic was a success. No complications. He is resting in his room. You are welcome to visit him now," the orderly recited.

"Wonderful news!" Fay exclaimed.

"Room four sixteen, ma'am," the orderly offered. "Have a good evening, ma'am." She went about her duties.

The four of them had it all: balloons, flavored seltzer

water, and even a frickin' teddy bear. Jody had taken a ration of crap for it. Fay thought it cute. She realized how close these hardened combat warriors and brothers were.

David chided Jody about the bear. "You got Julio a teddy bear? Dang, man, he's a guy!"

"Yeah, well, every time I was in the hospital," Jody said, "I got a bear from a girlfriend and/or my mom."

'How many times were you in the hospital, dude?" David teased.

"I raced dirt bikes in high school. And I played ice hockey."

"Carp," David replied. "I get it!"

Fay realized today, on her fortieth birthday anniversary, she was indeed a mom of three boys - or, if nothing else, something akin to a soccer mom.

Julio seemed thrilled, if a special forces warrior can be thrilled, to see everyone. He enjoyed the balloons and the ribbing he received for the bear.

"What are you going to name the teddy?" Fay inquired.

Julio looked at the bear and asked, "Is it a boy or a girl bear, Commander?"

Fay pretended to check the sex of the bear. "It's a lady bear," she proclaimed.

Huh," Julio said. "If it's a lady, then her name is David and Jody."

Anyone who could find a chair in the room had to sit. The laughter was so boisterous.

Chapter 14

One week later, JAG conference room
They had been chatting while waiting for their pretrial conclusion meeting when Fay entered the room.

Winslow first spotted her coming through the door. "Officer on deck!" he barked.

All in the room rose to assume the position of attention.

Fay smiled. "As you were," she said.

And they all sat.

"Okay, are we ready?" Fay asked all in attendance.

All agreed they were raring and willing to move forward.

"Julio, you are looking as fit as a fiddle," Fay said. "Don't worry, it's an old saying I used to hear my grandparents say. I don't know what it means either. But it sounds goofy enough."

Winslow picked up where he had left off with the pretrial formalities. "Military Rules of Evidence govern evidence submitted during the trial," he told the group. "Evidence the judge rules to be excluded by the rules are excluded from jury consideration."

"We have our finalists narrowed down to a reasonable group to select from," JP said.

"Thank you, Mrs. Fletcher," Winslow said. "A two-thirds vote is required to find you guilty. So, three of the five puts the odds in our favor. If at least three of the jurors cannot agree to the guilty verdict, you will be found innocent."

"I learned during my meeting last week with the JAG and Base Commander Wallace there will be a prosecutor detailed to represent the United States after all," Fay said.

Several people moaned. "It's okay, guys," Fay assured them. "We've got this."

"Do we know who the prosecutor is?" JP asked.

Fay searched through her pages of notes. "Marine Colonel Michelle Silver? I heard she is tough…I guess you would expect nothing less from a Marine?"

David smiled and commented, "You make a valid point, sir."

"Yeah, well, don't worry. I will figure her out," Fay said with confidence. She looked around the table and noted, "We are almost done."

Winslow picked it up. "We may have a chance to strike a deal with the prosecutor," he told the group. "Colonel Silver could agree to a less severe sentence if you agree to plead guilty. But the jury won't know about the deal. The idea is to give you a lighter sentence in exchange for proceeding with the court-martial."

David asked, "May I say something, sir?"

"Of course, David," Fay replied.

"Something I learned as a young black male growing up in the inner city about crimes and punishments: it's up to you; if you do a plea bargain, you for sure go to jail," David stated. "But the sentence is reduced and the time served is shortened. Today, ninety-eight percent of our incarcerated black brothers never went to trial."

"Geez!" Jody exclaimed. "How is that possible?"

"They plea bargain," David said. "So, for me, I will not bargain. We have great representation. I trust Commander Green and her team to do what is right for us."

Both Jody and Julio followed David's lead and also decided not to bargain.

"Excellent!" Fay said. "Okay, last thing. If you are asked to testify, make sure you remember what all we prepared for. A cross-examination by a Marine colonel is hard to take while still keeping your cool. Stick to your 'yes sirs' and 'no sirs' and 'I do not recall' - oh, and 'that's classified, sir' - and you will be golden."

"Thank you, sir," each man chined in.

"It is our honor to serve you," Fay said. "Now, get out of here and go do something fun."

Julio, David, and Jody rose from their chairs. They assumed the position of attention, and although military protocol did not require it, the men snapped a crisp salute.

Fay rose and returned their salutes. "Dismissed," she said respectfully.

Following the meeting, Fay, Winslow, and JP returned to their assigned offices. Fay needed to learn more about her opponent, Marine Judge Advocate Colonel Michelle Silver. Winslow and JP were set on the tasks of vetting the five jurors. They had two weeks until the trial.

Fay's research revealed the Colonel hailed from Salt Lake City, Utah, which could mean Silver was both of the Mormon faith and a Republican. Perhaps she was one, the other, or both. At the very least, she would be used to who they were. She had not attended BYU as Fay had, and Fay had lived her early years in the Mormon faith, until her grandmother took the family away from the Mormons and to the Methodist religion. It had been confusing for little Fay.

Colonel Silver had earned both her Bachelor's and Juris Doctor at Penn State. After college, she had enlisted in the Marine Corp as a lawyer, following much the same career path as Fay. Another thing both women had in common: they seldom lost a case. Silver was three years Fay's senior in age and had served in the Marines Corps for sixteen years.

****

08:00 hours, 13th Naval District conference room, Bremerton, the court-martial

Marine Colonel Silver began the proceedings. Silver stood facing Acting Judge Navy Admiral Brandon May. "The United States versus Sergeant Main, Sergeant Adams, and Sergeant Caitlin," Silver announced. "The accused are charged with manslaughter and conduct unbecoming."

Admiral May faced Commander Green. "Do the accused wish to enter a plea?" he asked her.

"They are not guilty," Fay declared.

"Enter a plea of 'not guilty,'" May said to the court recorder.

Fay had anticipated Colonel Silver would probe for their weakest point. Fay assumed this would be Jody. For the seating arrangement at the defense table, she had placed Jody to her left. Julio and David were at the other end of the table. Winslow and JP sat at a table behind the four of them.

JP and Winslow were seasoned trial Legalmen. They knew if the Colonel began picking at Jody, or any of the other two Marines, they were to manage their body language. Eyes forward, no notetaking, no whispering. No reaction.

Admiral May spoke to Colonel Silver. "On behalf of the United States government, are you prepared to make your opening statement?"

Colonel Silver began. "The U.S. government will prove that on October second, the three accused Marines did willfully murder their wives. Sergeant Main strangled his wife, Sergeant Adams drowned his wife in her bathwater, and Sergeant Caitlin strangled his wife. To be sure, all brutal acts and now these specific actions need to be reconciled with the military justice system." She continued, "The times of death were between the night of October first and October second. These facts are undisputed and what I have explained to you is what we will later learn to be accurate as we proceed today. I want you to be mindful Commander Green will try a little smoke and mirrors, if you will, in her attempt to persuade you these three Marines are as pure as the driven snow - American heroes. Don't be fooled as she twists and turns the facts in her attempt to craft these tragic events into a believable story. Make no mistake, she will try to snow you with a bit of misdirection and a bit of hocus-pocus. Be wary of her charms."

Colonel Silver turned to Admiral May and said, "Thank you, Admiral May."

It was now Fay's turn; talk about a tough act to follow. According to Colonel Silver, Fay and a snake charmer had many things in common. Fay directed her opening remarks to the jury.

"Good morning, gentleman," Fay began. "My legal staff and I want to thank you for allowing yourselves the opportunity to do what is right for these three brothers in arms and what is suitable for our country. I am Commander Faydra Green, JAG Corps. I have served as a JAG for thirteen years. My background includes studies at BYU and the University of Texas, where I earned my law degree."

She turned to the defense table. "I wish to introduce you to the three accused."

The three Marines stood and assumed the position of attention. To Fay, they looked better than sharp. Haircuts all around, Marine parade uniforms complete with spit-shined shoes. All poster boys, to be sure.

She began the introductions. "Sergeant Jody Main, First Special Forces Operational Detachment-Delta," Fay told the assembled group. "Next, Sergeant Julio Adams, First Special Forces Operational Detachment-Delta and Sergeant David Caitlin, First Special Forces Operational Detachment-Delta. All three men are among our finest. Much of what these men do day in and day out in their country's service is classified as top-secret code UMBRA. They will not be allowed by nature of their duty assignments to answer specific questions concerning any of their duty-related activities."

Fay moved away from the jury and a little closer to Colonel Silver. "You will learn Colonel Silver has little evidence," Fay said, "and what she does have could be laughable."

Fay moved back toward the jury. "Three women are dead, but these men were not willing participants," she went on. "I will repeat it, Sergeants Main, Caitlin, and Adams were not willing participants in the deaths of their wives. I will ask you to take a leap of faith when I say these three men are here today because they did what your country asked them to do, and tragically, the results were the deaths of those dearest to them. Thank you for your service, gentlemen."

"We have three witnesses," Admiral May said. "Colonel Silver, you may call your first witness."

Silver announced, "Special Agent Mr. Corry Markham, NCIS, please take the stand."

Corry made his way to the stand.

Silver instructed him, "Please raise your right hand. Do you swear to tell the truth and only the truth, so help you God?"

Markham swore, "I do."

Silver then said, "Please have a seat, Agent Markham."

Time for a preemptive strike. Fay rose. "Please excuse me," she said. "I will remind Mr. Markham to be mindful of national security reasons. Any potential Category Three information he may be privy to is not admissible or allowed here today."

"Thank you for the reminder, Commander Green," Judge May said. "All in attendance here today are so advised."

Silver spoke up. "Agent Markham, it goes without saying for one person to be tasked with the investigation of three deaths must have been daunting."

Markham agreed, "Yes."

Silver asked, "Did you go it alone or did you have support?"

"At the onset, JAG Corp assisted."

"Is it unusual to have JAG Corp assistance?" Silver inquired.

Markham answered, "Somewhat. But because of the uniqueness of the investigation, it was warranted."

Silver next asked, "Who from JAG Corps co-investigated?"

Markham replied, "Commander Green."

"You said at the onset of the investigation Commander Green assisted," Silver stated. "Can you tell us what happened?"

Markham responded, "My understanding is she was reassigned."

Silver remarked, "Huh. So, she was on the case, then she was off the case. Correct?"

Markham confirmed, "Yes. Captain Vernon Towsley, JAG Corps, relieved her."

"Agent Markham, you are a civilian serving in the NCIS?" Silver asked him.

"Most of the special agents are."

Silver addressed another question to Markham. "When you reviewed the autopsy reports, did anything out of the norm catch your attention?"

Markham replied, "Nothing seemed unusual to me."

"Other than three women all dying within in the same geographical location within only several hours of one another," Silver remarked.

Markham answered, "Well, yes."

"Did you notice anything else?" Silver pressed.

Markham replied, "Two were strangled, and one drowned."

"All three women were found and reported to Shore Patrol by their husbands," Silver stated. "Is this correct?"

Markham confirmed, "Yes."

Silver asked, "Were you first on the scene following each report?"

"No," Markham informed her. "Commander Green preceded me."

At this, Silver said, "Seems unusual a lawyer, and

not an SP or NCIS, would be the first to report."

Markham responded, "It was Sunday. The Duty Officer could not be located, and SP had difficulty finding anyone at NCIS, is my understanding. Commander Green had the watch at JAG Corp. Again, that is my understanding."

Silver continued her line of questioning. "When you first interviewed each man, I presume at the crime scenes, did all of the men seem distraught or remorseful about the fact their wives had died?"

Fay launched to her feet. "Objection, Agent Markham is not a qualified psychiatrist," she stated. "As such, his answers would be founded on speculation as to the assessments of our three Marines' behaviors."

"Sustained," Admiral May responded. "The jury will disregard the question."

Silver said, "Thank you, Admiral May." She turned her attention back to Corry. "Mr. Markham, when you interviewed Sergeant Main, did he mention his duty assignment before his return to Bremerton?" she asked.

Fay had correctly predicted the Colonel would focus her attention on Jody.

Markham answered, "Sergeant Main, along with the other two men, was asked this question. All responded the same: 'Top secret,' or 'classified.'"

Silver asked, "Why were the three Marines only charged with manslaughter, Mr. Markham?"

"We did not have enough evidence," Markham replied.

"Not enough evidence, Mr. Markham," Silver repeated. "Why?"

Markham responded, "There were no eyewitnesses, which left me looking for circumstantial evidence."

"Mr. Markham," Silver requested, "will you recap for the jury how each of the three women died?"

"Her husband found Cindy Adams drowned in a bathtub," Markham began. "The autopsy report confirmed her lungs were filled with water, indicating she may have been held under the water. Yet, there was no sign of a struggle. Marina Caitlin was strangled while she slept in her bed. She, too, had not fought for her life. It was as if both women willfully succumbed to death."

Silver remarked, "That is an interesting theory, Mr. Markham."

Markham resumed speaking. "On the other hand, Lisa Main was a scrapper. Her body was found on the living room floor; she, too, had been strangled. Evidence revealed Lisa had put up a fight. Death did not claim Lisa easily."

"Were each of the Sergeants examined for scrapes, cuts, or bruises?" Silver inquired.

Markham replied, "There were no indications. Sergeant Adams had two lacerations. One on his back and one on his thigh. My understanding is both wounds were received during his mission."

"Mr. Markham," Silver asked, "will you be available to this court-martial should we require additional testimony from you?"

"Of course," Markham promised.

Silver stated, "I have no further questions of our witness." Colonel Silver smiled. "Thank you for your time, Mr. Markham."

"Commander Green, would you like to interview our witness?" Admiral May asked.

"Yes, Admiral," Fay responded as she rose from her chair. Her eyes were locked on Corry as she proceeded to the stand. "Good morning, Mr. Markham," Fay greeted him. "I trust you are well?"

Markham replied, "Extremely well, Commander. And you?"

"I am doing great today, sir." Fay smiled. "I may have only two questions for you today, Mr. Markham. The autopsy reports indicated each woman had been bitten on the neck and on the breast," she stated.

Markham confirmed, "That is correct, Commander."

"On the neck? Like a vampire on the neck?" Fay asked.

A chuckle could be heard from several of the jury members.

Markham replied, "The necks had been bitten. Although there were no puncture wounds, if that is what you mean."

"What I am having trouble with, Agent Markham," Fay said, "is while I have three Marines on trial here today, I have three women who were all bitten on the neck and on the breast. Would that not suggest one person, not three, was responsible for these deaths?"

Markham answered, "I considered it."

"And your conclusion, Mr. Markham?" Fay pressed.

Markham responded, "I did not have enough evidence to draw a conclusion from."

"Mr. Markham, you, I, and Colonel Silver had access to the psychological evaluations of each Marine. Will you tell us your impressions?" Fay requested.

Silver spoke up. "Objection, Mr. Markham's opinion would not be qualified."

May ruled, "Sustained. Please withdraw the

question, Commander Green."

"I will rephrase," Fay agreed. "Concerning all three evaluations as a whole, did you notice anything unusual?" she asked Markham.

Markham answered, "Each evaluation was heavily redacted. They were of no use to me."

Fay replied, "Thank you, Mr. Markham. I have no further questions."

May then stated, "You are dismissed, Agent Markham. Ladies and gentlemen, we have had a lot to digest this morning. Let's take a fifteen-minute break."

Fay addressed her charges. "Okay, guys. Remember, if anyone asks a question, no comment. Right? Oh, and no one on cell phones. Okay?"

All nodded in agreement.

During the break, Fay and Winslow met with Jody. They told him to be ready to take the stand and to be cool and stick to the script. If he did as they said, he would be okay and nothing could happen to him.

Fay and Winslow walked along the hall back to the trial on their way from obtaining coffee and using the restroom. Near the door, on a bench, sat her three boys. In their dress uniforms, they looked as sharp as hell. But what took Fay's heart was the sight of three U.S. Marine Corps alpha males sitting with headphones in their ears, listening to music. It was ironic because these were Jon's men. They had found a solution to discourage anyone from asking them a question: the earphones. Fay felt pride, while at the same time, sadness; her boys had each lost a loved one. Whatever she had to do, even if it cost her her life, she vowed to make this right for these guys.

All returned, and the court-martial resumed. Fay had thought the doctor who had evaluated the three Marines would be next on Colonel Silver's list. Surprisingly, this was not so.

Silver said instead, "The government would like to call Marine Sergeant Jody Main to the stand."

Jody rose as he passed by Fay. She whispered, "You got this." She would have liked to be able to hold her breath for Jody's entire testimony.

Silver asked, "Sergeant Main, do you swear to tell the whole truth and nothing but the truth, so help you God?"

Main replied, "I do."

"You can be seated," Silver told him. "Sergeant Main, you are a member of the Marine Corps elite First Marine Raider Battalion, correct?"

"Yes, sir," Main confirmed. "We all are."

"How long have you been a Raider team member?" Silver asked him.

Main replied, "I don't recall, sir."

"After the time you returned from duty and up until the death of your wife, did everything seem okay between you and your spouse?" Silver inquired.

Main once again said, "I don't recall, sir."

Silver tried again. "You are close with your team members. Were Sergeants Adams and Caitlin getting along with their wives?"

Fay rose. "Objection," she stated. "This would be speculation on Sergeant Main's part."

"Sustained," Admiral May responded.

Silver resumed speaking. "Are you now, or were you up until the death of your wife, taking any medications? Legal or otherwise?"

Main responded, "No, sir."

Silver next asked, "Are you a bodybuilder? I would

imagine your hands are powerful."

Main agreed, "Yes, sir."

"And when you get angry, do you become angry quickly?" Silver inquired.

Main denied this. "No, sir."

"Your wife, Mr. Main. Does she come to anger quickly?" Silver wondered.

"Objection. Mrs. Main's temperament is not at issue here," Fay declared.

"Sustained," Admiral May replied.

Silver said, "Thank you, Sergeant Main. Your witness."

Fay spoke next. "Sergeant Main. How are you holding up? Can I get you a sip of water?" she asked him.

Main replied, "No, sir."

"I believe the judge, Colonel Silver, and my team have privy to your service record," Fay went on. "For the benefit of the jury, in your four and a half years of service, how many medals have you been awarded?" She hoped he would stray from the standard 'yes, no, I don't recall' litany."

Main answered, "Three, sir."

Fay responded, "Yes, I see them there now. And for the jury. Maybe one or two of them can't see so well; what are they?"

There were several chuckles from the jury area.

Main replied, "Sir, Distinguished Service Medal, awarded for exceptionally meritorious duty in the service of the United States government in a time of great responsibility."

"Go on, Sergeant Main," Fay encouraged him. "I am already impressed."

Main smiled. "Sir, Navy Commendation Medal,

awarded for heroic achievement or service, and the Purple Heart, sir. Sir, Sergeants Adams and Caitlin were also awarded the Purple Heart during the same mission."

"You were all wounded in combat, and none of you managed to duck for cover!" Fay said, loud enough for the entire court to hear. Again, chuckles from the jury. She even drew smiles from Admiral May and Colonel Silver. "I see a ribbon there as well," Fay observed. She already knew about the ribbon but wanted all in the room to hear about it, and, if the truth were to be known, she was on a roll.

Main replied, "The expert marksman ribbon, sir."

"I am very impressed. I am sure as your career continues in the U.S. Marine Corps, there will be more to come." Fay paused, then said, "But promise me no more Purple Hearts, okay!"

Main replied, "Yes, sir."

"You are dismissed," Fay told him.

Admiral May spoke next. "Let's take a noon recess. We will resume at 13:30 hours."

Fay wanted to keep everyone contained. JP arranged for a vacant room at the O-club and a lunch to be delivered. Fay also thought it best everyone spent at least a portion of their time outside for an O2 break.

During lunch, Fay asked Winslow and JP, "How is it going?"

"I think we are managing, sir," JP said.

"Is that good or bad?" Fay asked.

"It's good, sir," JP replied. "Colonel Silver isn't as scary as I thought she would be."

"I thought that as well. Either she is holding back and has a bombshell to drop on us. Or….?" Fay wondered.

"Or what, sir?" Winslow inquired.

"Or her heart is not in this," Fay speculated. "I mean, we have three Marine alpha dogs. All multiple medal winners. It is hard to tell where she is heading with this."

"Her unproductivity has us off balance," Winslow said. "Is that what you are thinking?"

"I believe so," Fay said. "She is competent. As I suspected, she went to Jody right away. Yet, she did not hit him as hard as she could have." Fay averted her eyes toward a nearby window. "I, or we, better figure it out soon, or we could get broadsided."

****

13:30 hours, the court-martial of the three Marines resumes

All were present waiting for the arrival of Judge Admiral May.

May entered the room. Someone barked, "Senior officer on deck!" All assumed the position of attention.

"At ease," May said. All returned to their seats. May then stated, "Order of business before we begin." He glanced around the room. "I am aware of the protocol as much as the next person. We have a lot on our tables this week, things more important than calling a room to attention every time an officer enters. Let's dispense with the distraction moving forward."

Jody, sitting next to Fay, said, "He's a good guy, sir."

Admiral May had had a hand in Fay's promotion from Lieutenant Commander to Commander the prior year. Fay replied, "Yes, he is."

"Colonel Silver, are you ready to call your first witness of the afternoon?" May asked.

Silver smiled and rose from her chair. "The

government would like to call Major Megan Schwartzman to the stand."

Major Schwartzman approached the stand and remained standing while Colonel Silver swore her in.

Silver asked, "Major, do you promise to tell the truth and nothing but the truth, so help you God?

Schwartzman responded, "I do."

"Thank you, Doctor. Please have a seat," Silver instructed. "Doctor, I'm more interested in the physical aspects of the three deaths. Did you perform the autopsies?"

Schwartzman confirmed this, saying, "My staff and I did, Colonel Silver."

Silver asked, "You signed the autopsy reports as the supervening authority, did you not?"

"I did," Schwartzman affirmed.

"It has been well established how the three women died," Silver went on. "The reports stated all three women were bitten on specific areas of their bodies."

Schwartzman verified, "That is correct."

Silver asked, "Will you tell us about the bites?"

"All three women sustained bites on their necks, breasts, and in Mrs. Caitlin's case, on her left heel," Schwartzman reported.

"Were the bites indicative of human bites, or another source?" Silver wondered.

Schwartzman said, "My staff and I believe they are human."

"You sound unsure, Doctor Schwartzman."

Schwartzman responded, "They are bites. We are sure."

"Were the marks consistent with those typically inflicted by a human being?" Silver inquired.

Schwartzman replied, "They appear to be human."

"Correct me if I am wrong," Silver said. "When a human bites into any flesh, a teeth pattern is left to record the biting. Is that correct?"

Schwartzman answered, "There often is."

"So, in these three cases, were you able to establish an identifiable tooth print, if you will?" Silver questioned.

Schwartzman answered, "We could not identify a recognizable pattern other than one commonality in all three marks. The one wound appeared on each woman's breast as the letter 'J.' We were not able to confirm if, in fact, it was indeed a bite."

Silver then said, "Doctor, I would like to enter your photos of those bites as evidence. You have six photos."

Schwartzman handed the photos to Colonel Silver. Silver reviewed them and passed them on to Admiral May. "The government would like these six photos entered in evidence," Silver stated. "Submitted and recorded today as exhibits A through F."

The photos were recorded and distributed to the jury for their perusal.

When the photos have been returned to the clerk, Silver said, "Doctor Schwartzman, thank you for your service." She directed her attention to Admiral May. "The government has no further questions, your honor."

"Commander Green, would you like to cross-examine the witness?" May asked.

Fay rose. "Thank you, your Honor," she said, approaching the stand. "Thank you for coming today, Major Schwartzman."

Schwartzman replied, "Thank you, Commander."

"Doctor, how long have you been involved with

forensic medicine?" Fay inquired.

Schwartzman replied, "Over twenty years, Commander,"

"The analysis of biting and the residual markings left on the human skin is an almost everyday occurrence for you?" Fay guessed.

Schwartzman said, "Yes, I could say so."

Fay then commented, "You stated you were not able to establish a distinguishing pattern on any of the three women's bodies."

Schwartzman confirmed this. "Yes."

"There would be no way to link any of the three husbands to these assaults by those bite marks?" Fay asked.

Schwartzman replied, "My staff and I could not make a connection in any of the three cases."

"Thank you, Doctor," Fay responded. "I have no further questions. You may be dismissed."

May said, "Thank you, Major Schwartzman. Ladies and gentlemen, let's take a fifteen-minute break."

Chapter 15

During the break, JP's curiosity got the better of her. "Fayzie, I noticed you have not been consuming your usual four gallons of coffee today," she said to her sister. JP wrinkled her brow. "Are y'all not feelin' well?"

"I am better than ever," Fay replied, taking a sip from a can of cola. "I found this stuff." She reached into her pocketbook and produced a small bottle. Showing it to JP, she said, "*Caffeine Plus*. It's pure caffeine, I think."

"And I suppose you are mixin' it with your cola?" JP guessed.

"Yep." Fay, with a look of satisfaction, added, "It works. And I am not dead yet."

JP shook her head, displaying her mock disgust. "I'm going to find Winslow and the guys. Do y'all know where they went?"

Fay pointed toward a nearby park. "Over there. Winslow had a football. I think they are playing catch?"

"Cool!" JP exclaimed. "I'm in!"

Fay looked at her wristwatch. "You got five minutes," she called after her sister. "And be careful!" Fay averted her gaze to the cola. Talking to herself, she commented, "I have become a full-blown mother. Haven't I?"

The court-martial resumed twenty minutes later.

When all had settled, Admiral May announced,

"Will the government call its next witness?"

Colonel Silver rose and stated, "The government calls Lieutenant Commander Marcus Garcia."

Lieutenant Commander Garcia approached the stand.

"Raise your right hand," Silver instructed him.

Garcia did.

Silver then said, "Do you swear to tell the whole truth and nothing but the truth, so help you God?"

Garcia replied, "I do."

"Lieutenant Colonel," Silver began, "you did a psychological evaluation of Sergeant Main, Sergeant Adams, and Sergeant Caitlin. Is this correct?"

Garcia confirmed, "That is correct. My findings are in my reports."

Silver started, "Doctor, in your opinion -"

Fay lurched to her feet. "Objection," she interrupted. "May I ask the court for a sidebar, sir?"

"Granted," May replied. "Will the defense and the prosecution come forward?"

The sidebar afforded the two lawyers and the judge privacy from those in the courtroom.

Fay spoke first. "Your Honor, I fear any discussion regarding the mental status of the three men charged may risk exposure of their top-secret UMBRA mission. Sir, we will be walking a thin line here."

"Explain, Commander," Admiral May said.

"Sir, you are aware the green table hearing I participated in several months ago centered around not only these men's mission but several others as well," Fay told him. "The table was conducted on a need-to-know basis. My fear is because Lt. Colonel Garcia and the majority of the court are not need-to-know, there could be information divulged by Doctor Garcia that could expose the overall intent of the men's mission."

Because Admiral May had assigned Fay to the green table, he was aware of the mission and its top-secret nature. May said, "Colonel Silver, I appreciate the government's requirement we explore and render here today what is just and fair for all parties concerned. I am going to ask we do our jobs yet remain mindful of the sensitive nature of Doctor Garcia's findings."

Silver replied, "Thank you for your clarification, your Honor."

Fay returned her seat behind the defense table while Colonel Silver returned to the witness stand.

Silver resumed speaking. "Doctor Garcia, did you evaluate each man using the same testing methods?"

Garcia affirmed, "Yes, Colonel. All clinical examinations were conducted under fair and unbiased conditions."

"Assuming what I might term 'an average and normal person,'" Silver went on, "did any of the three men's evaluations exhibit anything unusual to you?"

"Nothing out of the ordinary, Colonel," Garcia answered. "The three men have no recollection of the hours before the deaths of their wives."

Silver inquired, "Is this possible, Doctor?"

Garcia replied, "I considered it. I thought it possible the men were suffering from post-traumatic stress disorder."

"Would your testing reveal something abnormal if they were?" Silver wondered.

Garcia answered, "Yes."

"Your Honor," Silver said, addressing the judge, "I have no other questions for Lieutenant Colonel Garcia."

Silver turned to Fay. "Your witness, Commander."

Fay rose from her chair. She knew a potential landmine existed should Garcia get too deep into explaining how and why the three Marines could have acquired the capability to kill their wives. Fay did not know if Doctor Garcia was aware when *Deception Pass* had reassembled, it had teleported some of Roman Justine's frontal lobe, contaminating five of the six commandos' brains. Any speculation did not need to be heard by the jury.

"I have no questions, your Honor," Fay stated.

"Doctor Garcia, you are dismissed," May said. He glanced around the courtroom. "Colonel Silver, have you called all of your witnesses?"

Silver stood. "Yes, I have, your Honor."

"Thank you. At this time, we will adjourn for a break. The court will resume at 15:30 hours," May intoned. "Dismissed."

During the recess, Fay met with Winslow and JP. "What do you both think?" she asked them.

"The proceedings are moving fast," JP said.

"I wondered why Colonel Silver did not call David or Julio to the stand?" Winslow asked.

"I wondered about it too," Fay said. "Based on Jody's testimony, she may have reasoned she would only hear more of the same from David and Julio. Jody was her trial balloon. What she learned from him will determine which direction she takes concerning the other two."

Winslow offered, "I thought Jody did a great job on the stand."

"He is a rock star," Fay said. "I am so proud of him."

"The most damage to our defense could have been

Lieutenant Colonel Garcia," JP said. "Whatever occurred in the sidebar flat snuffed his testimony, it seems."

"Many questions regarding what we learned at the green table may have spilled out if he divulged too much in the way of incidental information," Fay told them. "Admiral May knew it, and I knew it. He did a great job of informing Colonel Silver not to go there without telling her why not to go there."

"Squelching Doctor Garcia's testimony pretty much took the air out of Colonel Silver's precaution, didn't it?" Winslow asked.

"One would think," Fay said. "No telling what the jury thinks. They can do strange and unpredictable things."

Following the break, the court reconvened.

Admiral May spoke, "Welcome back. We will begin closing statements. The government will go first, followed by the defense. Colonel Silver, if you are ready, you are up."

Colonel Silver stood, smiled at Admiral May, and said, "Thank you, your Honor." She turned and proceeded to address the jurors.

"Good afternoon," Silver began. "Thank you for being here with us today. Gentlemen, if we know anything, we know three women are dead. We know on behalf of their families, and for the sake of their souls, we must each make a decision today to do what is morally right."

Colonel Silver began pacing from one side of the box to the other. She continued to talk while at the same time looking each man in the eye. She appeared stern, and she seemed to be sympathetic to their onerous task at hand.

"Gentlemen, while our tasks are arduous, we know we will persevere because we are Marines." She stopped walking when she reached the president sitting at the right end. Looking into his eyes, Silver said, "Today, we will do what is right for the three loving wives, mothers, and daughters who lost their lives far too young. When the defendant was asked to recall the night of his wife's death, the responses were, 'I don't recall.'" The colonel began pacing again. "When asked about their mission, we heard, 'that is classified.' In the end, the defendant did not tell us anything. Did he? I, like you, understand the precepts of the 'need-to-know' military code. Secrets are what keep all of us from tyranny. I would surmise each of you gentleman holds a secret clearance at one level or another. As Marines, we understand this. But where does it stop, and where does the willingness to be honest begin? Here? Today?" Colonel Silver paused. She then said, "I do not know. I will leave it for you men to decide."

Colonel Silver walked to the prosecutor's table to take a sip of water, then she turned back to the jury. "I believe if I had spent the evening with my spouse, and they had died, I would know why," she went on. "Major Schwartzman's testimony and the testimony of NCIS Agent Markham indicated Mrs. Main, Mrs. Caitlin, and Mrs. Adams may appear to have been willingly strangled or drowned. One fought for her life. Why? Let's think about it," Silver mused. "Mrs. Adams willingly drowned? Unless someone is comfortable with another in an intimate setting, I would think there would be a fight for life. And in the case of Lisa Main, poor Lisa fought for her life. She knew her attacker."

As Fay listened to Colonel Silver, she could not help but think how Julio, David, and Jody must feel. Especially Jody. In Fay's mind, the three men were as innocent as she. Fay placed her hand on Jody's forearm in a gesture of reassurance.

"Gentlemen, you have a lot to weigh today," Silver stated. "I hope you will do what is right for three women, and you will do what is right for America." She looked each man in the eyes. "I wish to thank each of you today for your service." She turned and walked away.

It was Fay's turn. Admiral May looked in Fay's direction. "Commander Green," he asked, "do you wish to make a final statement?"

"I do. Thank you, your Honor." Fay proceeded to the jurors. She stood before the five jurors and smiled. "Thank you, gentlemen, for being here for these three men," she said as she pointed toward Jody, David, and Julio. "Each of you has been asked to take a leap of faith. You have been asked to set aside what might seem normal and trust in the integrity of your brothers in arms." Fay moved toward the jury president. "Mr. President, I ask when you meet in a few minutes to decide the fate of these three heroes, all of you will dig deep into your hearts to find the right verdicts today."

Fay turned toward Colonel Silver. "The prosecutor has made a few valid points," she conceded, "yet I will remind you only circumstantial evidence has been submitted. And, while it was established the three women were either strangled or drowned, all three exhibited one thing in common. The proof of bite markings, gentlemen. This would suggest one killer, not three, committed these crimes. The prosecutor has not established with certainty any of these three men assaulted their wives, resulting in their deaths."

Fay turned away from the jury toward David, Julio, and Jody. All of them had remained at attention throughout her summary. "A special forces designation means doing what is above and beyond the call of duty," Fay continued, "exceeding those things we all do as we go about our daily tasks in the service of our country. Often, missions deemed 'top-secret' or 'classified' take those who perform them beyond what is safe and sane with great risk of life. A risk many are not willing to take."

Fay walked toward Colonel Silver. Standing near to her, she faced the jury. "We all want what is fair and just," she said. "I ask you to give these brave men your deepest considerations today. Not guilty of all charges. Thank you." Fay returned to the defense table and stood at attention next to the three Marines.

"Mr. President," Admiral May said, "if you will begin your deliberation, you are dismissed."

The five jury members left the courtroom.

May said, "You are dismissed until the jury reconvenes."

The hallway outside of the courtroom was congested. Fay and her group found several benches near the entry door. When the jury reconvened, they would know it.

Jody asked Fay, Winslow, and JP their opinions. "How do you all think it went?"

Winslow and JP deferred to Fay. "I think it went well, guys," Fay said. "There is little in the way of evidence, and my opinion is the prosecution has a weak case."

"That's good news, right?" said David.

"In a way," replied Fay, "but there are many facets to this, making even what is simple more complex. We have five jurors who do not think alike. They each heard something different. We also have several options for their verdict. All of you could be found innocent and returned to active duty. Or all found innocent but suspended or relieved of duty. There are three of you, which means each of you could receive a different verdict."

"Could you make a prediction, sir?" Julio asked.

"Let's be optimistic and hope for the best-case scenario," Fay said. "I have a good win-loss record. I seldom lose. It does not mean the verdict is not one hundred percent in my favor. So, the win is sometimes a compromise. What makes this so difficult to predict is the unpredictability of the jury. Let's be positive! A one hundred percent win all the way around."

"On behalf of all three of us, thank you, sir," David said.

Forty-five minutes passed before it was announced it was time for all to return to the courtroom. The jury had reached its decision.

As Fay passed by Winslow and JP, who were standing together, she whispered, "Uh-oh." She knew a short deliberation could spell trouble.

When Fay passed through the courtroom door, from the corner of her left eye, she noticed Jon Shaman, the three Marines' team leader, sitting alone in the back row. Jon, a ghost, was risking a lot by being there for his men today. She knew Jody, David, and Julio saw him as well. It was a great morale booster for the three Marines. Although Fay did not look at Jon, her hands were at her side when she wiggled the fingers on her left hand. He would notice her subtle wave.

Everyone sat, and the jury waited until Admiral May had entered the room and taken his place behind his bench.

"Mr. President," May said, "I understand you have a verdict."

The jury president rose, responding, "We have, your Honor."

"Will the defendants please rise for the verdict?"

Julio, Jody, David, Fay, Winslow, and JP all rose to receive the jury's verdict.

The jury president handed a sheet of paper to the court clerk, who passed it to Admiral May. The president sat.

As Admiral May read the verdicts, Fay watched for a facial response from Admiral May. There was none.

May averted his eyes from the paper and said to the jury, "So say you all?"

Each member responded, "Yes."

To Fay, time moved almost backward as she waited with excruciating anticipation.

Admiral May read aloud from the paper. "Marine Sergeant David Caitlin, the jury recommends on the charge of manslaughter...not guilty." A quiet gasp could be heard throughout the entire room. May continued. "For the charge of conduct unbecoming...not guilty."

Fay felt her smile go from ear to ear. One down, two to go.

May continued. "Marine Sergeant Julio Adams, the jury finds on the charge of manslaughter...not guilty and for the charge of conduct unbecoming, also not guilty."

Only Jody remained. They were not of the woods yet but looking favorable.

"Sergeant Jody Main, the court finds…." May paused. He asked the court clerk to approach the bench. A discussion ensued, revolving around something written on the paper. When the matter finally appeared to be clarified, May continued. "Sergeant Jody Main, the court finds you not guilty in charge of manslaughter. As for the charge of conduct unbecoming, the court finds…not guilty."

Who could help but not cheer a unanimous verdict? Things seemed good, but Admiral May had yet to sentence the three men. He could order many options, up to and including discharge from the Marine Corps. He could choose different sentences for each man.

Admiral May addressed each man individually. "Sergeant Caitlin," he began, "the Marine Corps thanks you for your outstanding service. This court orders you are to return to active duty immediately with no loss of pay."

David remained at attention. His smile lit up the room.

"Sergeant Julio Adams," May said next, "the court orders you are to return to active-duty status immediately and with no loss of pay."

Last but not least, Jody was on deck. Fay grasped Jody's arm.

"Sergeant Jody Main, the court orders a thirty-day restriction from active duty," May announced.

Fay knew this was where it could go bad for Jody. He faced demotion in rank, at the worst.

May continued, "Following restriction from duty, you are to return to active duty at full rate and pay."

It did seem unusual Jody was sentenced differently from the other two men. Nonetheless, overall, this was a great win for the three Marines, the United States of America, and her and her team. Fay turned to see Jon's reaction. He, her ghost and assassin of choice, had disappeared. Fay was unsure if this win would be an occasion for celebration. Three deaths had occurred, yet she felt the need to debrief with her boys. She opted to dine at a nearby popular eating establishment. She asked Winslow to arrange for a private dining room there.

Outside of the courtroom, Fay broke from the group and proceeded to walk to her car. As she walked, thinking about all that had happened, she heard quick-paced footsteps approaching her from behind.

"Commander Green!" a voice said.

Fay stopped. She turned to greet Colonel Silver, her adversary. Fay smiled and welcomed her. "Colonel, thank you for stopping me."

"I hoped you and I would get the chance to meet before I left town, Commander," Silver said.

Fay had not lost her radiant smile. "My honor, Colonel," she replied. "My friends call me Fay." Fay had yet to learn if Silver was a hostile loser or not.

Colonel Silver smiled, an encouraging sign anyway.

"Fay, I wanted to congratulate you and to thank you," Silver said. She extended her hand. "My friends and friends call me Shelly."

"Shelly, I am honored to have served with you for the past two days."

"And I as well, Fay," Silver answered. "You know, it may sound strange, but this one I am happy to lose. I never will understand why the jury acquitted. Someone died." Silver hesitated and added, "The right thing happened today. Didn't it?"

"Yes, it did," Fay agreed.

"Then I feel right about it," Silver declared. "I am going to go home and enjoy the weekend with my family."

"Something did occur. My guess is the NCIS will assign a cold case detail to pursue this matter," Fay surmised.

"Fay, I, like you, am a curious creature," Silver remarked. "I know top-secret, classified, and need-to-know as well as any. May I ask, did the mission indirectly have something to do with the three wives' deaths?"

With the slightest affirmative nod of her head, Fay winked and said, "Need-to-know, Shelly."

Shelly grinned, offered her hand to Fay, and said, "I hope we meet again, Fay."

Fay made it as far as her car when her cell phone blew up. Three texts were waiting. She opened each in order. The first was from Jon, who had finally learned how to text, unlike when she had first met him. His message displayed a smiling thumbs-up emoji. Fay threw her head back and laughed. One just had to know Jon the way she did to appreciate his text.

The next text was from her boss, Captain Vern Towsley: *I am so proud of you, Faydra*. The message was accompanied by a happy face emoji. The third text proved the most surprising and the most special. It was a message from Carson: *Faydra, you were you. So proud. Love, Carson*. His text was followed by several hearts and happy face emojis. Yet, Fay wondered how Carson knew the trial's outcome and how he had responded so quickly. He was somewhere nearby. This was all that mattered to her.

Chapter 16

JAG Corps, Bremerton, Washington, two days later
"Ma'am," Petty Officer Winslow said, "Admiral May is on the phone for you."

May was the Commander of Naval Special Warfare Command; who was she to keep the man waiting?

"Thanks, Don," Fay said. She shut the door between her inner and outer office. "Hello, Commander Green speaking," she said into the phone.

"Commander, Brandon May. Have you a minute?"

"Of course, sir," Fay replied. "How can I help?"

"Faydra, I am in Bremerton this week. Will you meet me?" May requested.

"Of course. When and where, sir?"

"Sorry for the short notice," he apologized. "Would this afternoon work?"

"Aye, sir." Fay looked at her daily calendar. It was wide open. "Two hours, sir? 16:30 hours?" she suggested.

"We can make it work. Conference room in the district office."

"Yes, sir. Conference room, 16:30," Fay confirmed.

May operated out of the Pentagon, yet he had remained in Bremerton following the court-martial. Fay stopped to inform JP about the conference room meeting with Admiral May on her way from her office.

Fay arrived first at the conference room. May was a

busy guy. It did not surprise her he might be running late. Not too long after, she heard a conversation outside the conference room door. Shortly after, the door swung open. Admiral May entered, along with a man she had not seen since her adventure in South Korea.

She stood at attention. "Gentlemen," Fay greeted them. "Welcome!"

Captain James Rayzon spoke first. "Commander Green!" He extended his hand. They shook.

"James! So good to see you!" Fay then smiled again, extending her hand. "Admiral May," she said to the other man. "Good to see you, sir."

May responded, "Commander Green. Thanks for meeting us."

This would not be a social call. Captain Rayzon, like May, was attached to NSWC. They wanted her to do something for them.

"Everyone, please be seated," May offered.

Fay had seen May not too long ago. She spoke to Rayzon. "James, how very good to see you. How have you been?"

"Exceptionally well, Faydra." He smiled. "Thank you for representing our team at courts-martial. We are more than pleased to have the men back on E-Team."

Fay had not known Jody, David, and Julio were E-Team; she had suspected it. When she had last seen James, he and his team had run a mission that had almost cost her her life. They had dove on the wrecked U. S. S. *Jonathan Carr*, sunk by the North Koreans. With the aid of a SEAL and two Navy dolphins, Fay had located a code containing Russian/North Korean ballistic missile swap coordinates. She had become trapped in the ship, had managed to escape, and was only saved from drowning by the two dolphins, Juliet and Romeo, and the SEAL. It was something she never wished to re-experience.

Captain Rayzon spoke. "Faydra, we want you to join E-Team."

Fay had known something was up. She had not fathomed it would include her, a lawyer, a detective, and a woman, now being offered one of twelve spots on the most exclusive and secret special operations team in the military: E-Team or "Executive Detachment." The twelve team members reported to Admiral May. May, in turn, reported to President Ross.

"We aren't going to insult your intelligence, Faydra," May said. "The mission we want you to join is specific to you. We are hoping you will accept. Yet, this will be a duty assignment. You will understand once we explain."

"Thank you, sir," Fay replied. What else could she say?

"We will be going to *Deception Pass*," James began. "You are aware of her teleporting capabilities?"

Fay nodded. Although, from the onset, this did not sound encouraging. James Rayzon had led her last and only mission, a highly secret and highly dangerous one.

James continued. "A six-member team led by me. You will know the other four men: Petty Officers Lawrence and Valentine, Sergeant Wu, and Captain Shaman, plus you and myself."

Shaman? A SEAL, again! A captain? Mercy! So little do I know?! Fay thought to herself. Aloud, she said, "All good men, James. I will be honored to serve with them." May and Rayzon had said she could not decline. All that remained to be told was what she was going to risk life and limb for.

"Not only is *Deception Pass* capable of tele-transport, but she also has a limited capability of time travel." James paused. "I am going to allow it to sink in, Faydra," he told her.

Fay remained silent. If she started asking questions at this juncture, they would be there until midnight answering them. Perhaps they could answer her top five? "Gentlemen, I have several questions," she began. "I have accepted teleporting. I have accepted it as fact. Since I was a child, I have been aware of the thousands of bestselling science fiction novels and award-winning films and TV programs dealing with time travel. For those reasons, the logic in my brain will accept it as a possibility." Fay paused to collect her thoughts.

"Our experience with traveling in time has been in short duration," May said. "Months, rather than years."

"I suppose that's comforting," Fay acknowledged. "We are not going back to World War Two to prevent something major from occurring?"

"No," James replied. "We know the present is the present. It's fixed and does not change. There would not be anything we could do to change the present as we now experience it."

"I could not go back and trigger an event, like kill myself?" Fay wondered.

"No, you are still here now, talking to us," May said.

"If we are not going back to change an event, what are we, or what am I, doing?" Fay asked.

"Your nemesis, Roman Justine, and his companies were involved in improving the science of teleportation. His companies invested millions in the development of transporting," James said.

"When I am in the past Justine is not going to get me then, James?" Fay wanted to know.

"No," James reassured her. "He is dead, and you are alive."

May said, "We removed Justine from the Chinese prison to prevent him from making them aware the technology exists. Teleportation is a protected secret exclusive to the United States and Russia."

James picked up the briefing. "We learned Justine was preparing to sell his knowledge to the Chinese," he told Fay. "His death might have prevented it from happening. We reason there exist documents, technical schematics, or plans he planned to sell. We wish to find and retrieve them before the Chinese find them."

"When I travel back, will I travel as me or as Faye King?" Fay asked. "Justine eventually saw through my disguise. And he had sicked his hitman, Evilenko, on me."

"You would travel as Faye King," James said. "In the event you run into Inspector Popov, you might find it difficult to explain why there are two of you."

"I recall while I had lunch with Lavrov, he mentioned he saw a woman he thought looked like me observing us," Fay remarked. "I did not see her. If I were watching me, why don't I recall it? Why don't I recall any of the time from the trip I took to Moscow?"

"We believe the transition back to the present affects the traveler's memory," May explained. "You know Julio, David, and Jody experienced a brain alteration when *Deception Pass* materialized in the Yellow Sea."

"When we arrive at Saint Petersburg, we will set our plan into motion," James said. "JAG Corps will be advised of your temporary duty assignment."

"What will the duration of my duty assignment be?" Fay inquired.

May responded, "The travel time to *Deception Pass* and the travel time back. I think one week."

"And the time I am in Moscow?"

"Because you are in the past, and although you may spend a week or two there, you will return to the present at the same instant you left," May responded. "The result is no time lost."

"And I won't end up with a part of another's brain?" Fay had to know. "Similar to what David, Jody, and Julio experienced?"

"That was unusual," May said.

"Am I the guinea pig?" Fay asked next. "Or have others preceded me?"

"It has been tested without consequence," James assured her.

Fay rose, proceeding to the coffee maker. She started a brew. While waiting for the coffee, she asked, "Would either of you like a cup?"

Both men responded, "No, thank you."

"When do we depart?" Fay queried.

May replied, "In three days. *Deception Pass* is sailing for Saint Petersburg. E-Team will meet her en route. Once your op has been planned, you and the team will travel to Moscow, arriving one day before you arrived the first time."

"Oh, I have another question," Fay spoke up. She had a hundred more, yet this one was important. "When we first became aware of E-Team, my Legalman and I determined the team members have code names associated with Jesus's twelve apostles: James, Simon, David, Andrew, Matthew, Phillip, and, may he rest in peace, Paul." Fay smiled. "I have a code name, don't I?" She hoped so. When she had been First Daughter, her mom, dad, JP, and she had all had Secret Service concocted code names. She had been "Spirit," and her sister had been "Energy."

May looked at James. They both grinned. James replied, "Mary."

Fay laughed. "I thought so!"

****

U.S.S. Deception Pass, Baltic Sea, three days later

Mission planning began in the *Deception Pass* wardroom. Captain James Rayzon laid out the op. "This afternoon, we will teleport to a secure location in Saint Petersburg harbor," he said. "We will arrive five weeks from today at the minute of our departure. We are running a joint U.S.-Russian op. A Russian chopper will pick us up and will transport us to Kubinka Airbase near Moscow. You have all been issued U.S. passports and tourist vias. We will conduct the mission in civies. You have rubles, U.S. currency, and a credit card. We have booked reservations at a downtown hotel near Red Square."

Phillip asked, "What will our weapons be?"

"We are going in light," James said, "The standard HK Mk 23. The suppressors will be too bulky but at three pounds loaded, you will not be too restricted. And the weapon will be easy to conceal." James glanced around the room. "Questions?"

Phillip asked, "Do we expect trouble?"

"We are tourists. Our purpose is to secure Mary at all times," James told him. "We will operate in two-man teams. One team on each side of Mary's room and one team across the hall. In effect, Mary is surrounded."

"I am free to move about Moscow as I see fit?" Fay asked.

"Yes, your objective is to find Roman Justine's schematics before the Chinese do."

"And I have no idea where to look," Fay commented.

"You have a special skill at finding things," James said. "You found the codes, on the *Carr*, underwater, and in the dark. You quickly found the remains of Admiral Joe underwater while at the same time battling gators and sharks."

The last comment caused Fay to blush.

"Someone will have eyes on you twenty-four seven," James promised her.

****

23:00 hours, U.S.S. Deception Pass, Baltic Sea

Fay was resting in her bunk when a knock came at her door. She sprang from the bunk, reached for the door, and opened it.

"Time to go, ma'am," Andrew said.

"Thanks, Andrew," Fay replied. "Let me get my gear."

The two proceeded along a series of passageways then arrived at a large room. Rows of chairs at the center were arranged in airliner seating. Except for the seats, the room was otherwise barren. The staff wore white lab coats. Fay recalled Jon talking about the "tech-geeks." This must be them.

Andrew said, "Let's find a seat."

During the next several minutes, the other E-Team men came into the room and seated themselves.

Fay thought the geeks curious. Jon had told her he had conversed with one. He had come away from the conversation feeling they might be androids. While it was possible, they looked life-like. However, they lacked a human quality. Jon had said they had seemed not to have a personality. Fay agreed. Yet, she wondered if perhaps the geeks had been teleported enough times that whatever gave humans a personality had been erased. She hoped not. Perhaps it was better if the geeks were androids?

The process seemed much like preparing for flight departure. Seat belts were fastened, the difference being the belts were the same as those used in racing vehicles. They fastened crossing the chest. James and Andrew were seated on either side of Fay.

James said, "There will be a countdown. At zero, the ship will teleport. You won't realize anything has happened, although you may experience a feeling similar to motion sickness. The attendants will give us a shot before the countdown. It is supposed to counter the effects of travel. You will know if we gained or lost any time. Watch the timing display on the wall. At zero, if it is still counting, then we have successfully transitioned without time loss or time gain."

"But we will have arrived in the past?" Fay asked. "James, I have been bothered. How is it known that when *Deception Pass* arrives in Saint Petersburg harbor, there is not another object, a ship, not already occupying the space?"

James said, "It almost happened when *Deception Pass* arrived at the rendezvous point, which caused the collision between *Davidson* and *Vazhny.* To answer your question, radar is still functional. *Deception Pass's* auto-pilot nav systems can maneuver her to an occupied point."

"Which is why the teleport is performed at night," Fay realized. "To not scare the crap out of someone when it suddenly materializes."

"You got it, Faydra," James replied.

The geeks finished administering the shots. The team buckled in, preparing for the transport.

The countdown began: *ten nine…eight…* When the count reached zero, Fay experienced the headache to end all headaches, as if she had been drinking straight shots of vodka for several hours nonstop. The experience proved horrible.

All of the team unbuckled themselves but remained sitting, waiting to regain their bearing. The geeks circulated among the crew, again administering injections. When Fay received hers, the headache disappeared.

The team stood, retrieved their gear from storage lockers, and proceeded to the ship's helo pad. A Russian chopper, guided by the ship's crew, was landing on the pad when they arrived. The chopper's engines remained running as the team ran to an open door. The Russian Navy crew helped them board. Once they were all aboard and buckled in, the large chopper lifted from the pad and flew away.

The flight to the Russian base near Moscow would take around four hours, James told her. A few of the team were chatting, a few sleeping, or listening to music through headphones. Fay stared through the window of the chopper. Her mind was filled with a thousand questions. How would she find the schematics? Would she meet herself, and what would she say if she did? *"Hi, me, how are you?"* And what about the geeks? Who were they? What were they? Whatever they were, something in their manner seemed odd. Yet, she could not shake the feeling she had traveled back in time and somewhere out there, another her roamed.

****

05:30 Hours, New Rossiya Hotel, Moscow, Russia

The team checked in. After agreeing to meet in James's room at 09:30 hours, they retired for the night. Before she had departed from Bremerton, the FBI makeup team had recreated Faye King. They were so adept at it, Fay did not recognize herself. Indeed, the guys were still trying to wrap their minds around the transformation.

An hour later, Fay had not yet unwound. Her mind would not let her sleep. Finally, she got up and raided the mini bar, downing two tiny bottles of rum. It did the trick.

Chapter 17

Crazy Russian dance *muzak* blasting in her ear awoke Fay at 09:00 hours. She was in a rush to get to James's room for the 09:30 meeting. She knocked on the connecting interior door. Andrew opened the door. She entered into a room of laughing men. It appeared to her someone had told a joke.

"Morning, Mary!" James welcomed her, making light of her new commando code name.

"Hi, guys!" Fay replied. "I must have missed something funny."

Kimo (aka Phillip Wu) said to Fay, "I told the guys I never drink coffee. Until today. I've had three cups." Kimo again chuckled. "So, Andrew said, 'You must have gotten Commander Green's coffee addiction in a brain scramble when we teleported.'"

Fay laughed. "You know, come to think of it, I have not thought about coffee since we arrived in the past. Huh?" She leveled her eyes at Kimo and deadpanned, "Kimo, along with this new coffee addiction, did you also sit when you peed this morning?"

At her remark, the floodgates of laughter opened up.

It took several minutes for those in the room to contain themselves.

Fay said, "No, guys, just so you know, I have not lost my caffeine addiction. Nor did I stand when I peed this morning."

Following another round of hilarity, James said, "We have ordered a room service breakfast to your room, Mary. When it arrives, we will move the breakfast here."

Shortly after, there came a knock at Fay's door. "Room service!" a voice called.

Fay returned to her room. A few minutes later, she returned, wheeling a large cart of food. "This is a ton of food," she remarked. "Because it came to my room, does it mean I am paying for this?" Fay noticed there was nothing happier than a team of commandos come chow time.

While they ate, James added additional information to their upcoming op. "There will always be two of you with all eyes on Mary throughout the day," he told the team. "Between the six of us, we will plan the logistics - where and when."

Timmy (aka Andrew Lawrence) asked, "Are we running twenty-four seven rotations?"

"No," James said. "PDSS, the special purpose *Spetsnaz* unit of the Russian Naval Infantry in uniform, will handle all entry doors twenty-four seven. There will be non-uniformed men and women watching our hallway at night. We got the day shift, lads."

Kimo looked at Fay. "I guess it's up to Mary when she is good to go."

Fay replied, "Give me about an hour, guys, to think out my first day. I will notify y'all via headsets when I am on the move."

All agreed.

Fay returned to her room. It was time to think. She did her best thinking prone but instead chose to sit at the table near the window. Coffee was required for this. Her usual coffee cups were twice the size of the average cup.

There were no double-wide cups to be had. She instead poured two cups. She had no clue where to begin her hunt for the needle in the haystack. Heck, she first had to find the haystack before she gave any thought to finding the needle. She started jotting down notes.

I know I will not meet with myself, she wrote. *Otherwise, the other me would remember it. Probable, not Jon. He has enough to do keeping track of me already. Sasha is aware of Deception Pass's teleporting capabilities.* Fay sipped at her coffee. She made a sour face.

As she peered at the coffee, she commented out loud, "What the hell is this crap? Moscow's Worst Coffee?" Her home favorite was nothing like this. Cream and sugar were needed.

She continued to write: *Sasha will be the most logical to ask for help. He saw me when we were having lunch at the Ritz Carlton. And perhaps Katrinka, Sasha's supposed daughter? And I know I do not want to have anything to do with Popov. He won't recognize me. What about Roman Justine? I have to watch out for him. He by now knows Faye King and Fay Green are both me. Another one to be wary of is Evilenko. He knows my duo likeness. Irishka is going to assassinate him within the next few days. He's taken care of.*

Sasha would be first on her list. She knew his cell number and where they were meeting at the Ritz Carlton. If she went to the Ritz, she could alert him she was in town. Fay grabbed her pocketbook and pistol, and then put on her coat, sunglasses, and a hat.

Next, she contacted James using the headset system they had opted to use. "I'm going out to find Lavrov," she told him.

In turn, James contacted the team using the same system. "Mary is on the move," he informed them.

Fay arrived at the Ritz Carlton in time to see Inspector Popov leave and Sasha enter. She followed him in. He did not notice her. While past her and Sasha were busy greeting one another, she slipped around behind them, taking a position behind a large plant. It seemed odd, her watching herself from afar. *This must be what it's like to have a twin. But both sharing the same brain*?

Fay had not realized she was as flirtatious as her past self now appeared. Yet, she had never been accused of not being charming. She waited through the lunch order, and Sasha did look in her direction. This would have been when he had told her not to turn around and that he had seen someone who resembled her observing them. She knew that next, her past self would excuse herself to retire to the restroom. She would have a few minutes to contact Sasha. Past Fay stood, excused herself, and walked away.

Fay immediately walked to their table and sat. The many looks on Sasha's face were priceless. "Sasha, it's me, Fay," she told him.

"You were in the restroom for thirty seconds. You changed that quick?" he gasped.

"No. It's me from the future," Fay explained. "I've come back in the past. Sasha, I do not have time. I will be back in a minute, and I don't want me to see me."

Sasha was an intelligent guy. He picked things up fast. "*Deception Pass*?" he guessed.

"Yes," Fay confirmed. "After lunch, you and I are going to visit dead Lenin and then visit the Tomb of the Unknown Soldier. You will walk me back to the Ritz

Carlton. Afterward, meet me at the Grand Café Dr. Zhivago. I will explain everything." Fay spotted her past self exiting the restroom. She stood. "I'm coming back. Gotta go." She quickly left.

Fay waited for Sasha at the café. She had not seen any of her team, but she guessed they, like Jon Shaman, were good at blending in. Sasha entered through the café's entrance and paused while he seemed to readjust his mind to accept her. He spotted her, smiled, and proceeded to her table. She stood and embraced Sasha. She had not seen or spoken to him since their meeting weeks ago in Moscow. They sat.

"I know you have more questions than I have answers," Fay told him. She smiled. "How have you been?"

"I was doing good, Faya, until about two hours ago," Sasha remarked.

"I had to come here," Fay said. "I must have seen the film *Doctor Zhivago* twenty times since I was a child. Boris Pasternak, David Lean, Omar Sharif, and Julie Christie. What an epic love story."

"You remind me of Julie Christie, Faya," Sasha complimented her.

Fay's smile widened. "Why, thank you, sir! So I have been told. Yet, the film was made around nineteen sixty-five?"

"True. Actors do not change. They are frozen in time. And apparently, you are too."

"I am sorry, Sasha," she apologized. "My intent was not to shock."

"No, no. I in the future will recall this did happen," Sasha reassured her.

"You will," Fay said. "Can I order something light?

I have not eaten since this morning."

Sasha called the waitperson. He looked at Fay. "How about a hamburger?"

"A hamburger? Yeah, why not?" she decided.

The waitperson noted the order and left.

"The other you had a noteworthy lunch, not more than a few hours ago," Sasha commented.

"It was a lunch to remember," Fay said. "Thank you again. And, although I did not have room to pack it, I still treasure the Red Moscow. It is for my extraordinary occasions only."

Sasha reached across the table and clasped Fay's hand. "It is good to meet you again, and what can I do for you?" he asked.

"I have returned via teleport and time travel aboard *Deception Pass*," Fay said. "You knew about her capabilities to teleport but were you aware she could make short-time trips as well?"

"I was not," Sasha admitted. "I am not surprised, either."

"I have arrived with a team of six U.S. commandos like those who were previously aboard *Deception Pass*," Fay went on. "Now, it is feared Justine will sell the teleporting technology he has developed to the Chinese. I am here to acquire the technology before the Chinese do."

Sasha sat back. He tapped a spoon on the table while he let her words sink in. "You have a plan?" he guessed.

"I do not know where to begin. I am told I have an uncanny ability to find things. I am going to go with that," Fay replied.

The waitperson arrived with a huge hamburger. Everything in Moscow was huge. The largest bell and cannon in the world were parked in the Kremlin. The largest airplane in the world, the Antonov An-225, carried cargo around the world.

"The documentation would be stored on thumb drives, would they not?" Sasha guessed.

"I think the same," Fay agreed. "A safe is locked in Justine's office. I don't know where it is."

The waitperson walked by the table. Sasha stopped her. "Coffee, please," he requested.

"I hope what you ordered is better than what I drank this morning," Fay joked.

Sasha smiled. "Two coffees," he said to the waitperson. "This will be better."

"Thank you, Sasha. I seem to have cut back on my coffee consumption of late." Fay went on. "My first plan will be to find Justine's office, then break in. It most likely has an alarm or surveillance system. Find the safe and break into the safe and get out before I get caught. I would think the penalty for breaking and entering in Moscow comes with a hefty fine and penalty?"

"I think fine and work camp," Sasha confirmed.

"If I had diplomatic immunity?"

"It is an idea I will look into this afternoon. As long as you do not kill someone," Sasha responded. "I will find it out."

Fay had learned this from Popov at the airport back before she had boarded the Air Serbia flight with Jon Shaman to Belgrade. He had let her go. Katrinka had come along with a handy alibi, and Popov had gone home with his tail between his legs.

"It is possible President Ross has alerted President Rudkovsky I am here," Fay told Sasha. "It would explain why we were allowed to park *Deception Pass* in Saint

Petersburg Harbor, as well as the pickup from the Russian Navy chopper and the Russian Naval Infantry at the hotel entrances."

"It makes sense," Sasha said. "I will have someone tail Justine. We find out where his office is. We have the best safecracker and computer hackers in the world. I will have them stand by. When you are ready, you tell me."

The waitperson served the coffees. "May I serve you anything else?" the waitperson asked.

Fay had been picking at her hamburger during the conversation. It was more than she could handle. She said to the waitperson, "Will you wrap it up to go?"

"Of course," he said.

Before the waitperson left the table, Sasha asked him to wait. "Faya, would it help if you had a glass of special wine to calm your nerves?" he asked her.

"A great idea, Sasha." Fay accepted.

Sasha spoke to the waitperson in Russian. The waitperson then left the table.

"When we locate Justine's office," Fay told Sasha, "I will have to find a way to distract him away from the office in sufficient time to allow me to search it."

"I know Justine has a weakness for young women," Sasha recalled.

"It is true," Fay confirmed. "We call men like this 'perverts' in America."

"We have pervert here. I think Katrinka can distract Justine for you," Sasha offered.

"Little Katrinka! What!" Fay gasped. "Sasha, she is your daughter!"

Sasha's lack of a response clued her in, as well as the smile on his face.

"Katrinka is not your daughter?" Fay guessed.

"Katrinka is 'honey pot' spy," Sasha confirmed. "You call her 'Sparrow.'"

"Oh, that is sad," Fay remarked. "She is a sweet girl."

"Not to worry about Katrinka. She is not a sex spy, and she is capable agent," Sasha reassured her.

"I don't know if I feel better about it or not," Fay replied.

"She will be okay, Faya. She is good at her job. She will keep Justine busy for you." Sasha paused as if he were debating with himself, then he spoke again. "Are you ready for a history lesson I promise will blow up your mind?"

Chapter 18

"Go for it, Sasha," Fay prompted. "I am all ears."

Sasha had a quizzical look on his face. "What is 'all ears?'" he asked, confused.

Fay explained, "It means all of my attention is focused on you and your history lesson."

"Oh." Sasha did not seem sure about her explanation. "Okay," he said anyway. "I will tell you about Katrinka. She told you what she must do to support parents. Her skills were exceptional and gained the attention of some military men. They sent her to spy school for the Sparrow."

"Yes, she did tell me some of her stories," Fay recalled. "I am heartbroken."

"Good news is it gets better," Sasha said.

"Thank God."

"When Katrinka become nineteen years, I met her. It seemed to me she deserved better life. So, I introduced her to people at Kremlin," Sasha recounted. "A decision was made to bring her to the Main Directorate of the General Staff of the Armed Forces of the Russian Federation, abbreviated GU, formerly the Main Intelligence Directorate. She was assigned to Irishka for training. They are very close."

"She became a spy," Fay interrupted. "Sorry, go on."

"It was best thing for her, but at same time, GU

assignment is dangerous. But at least she had government protection." Sasha paused, sipped at his coffee, and continued. "I adopted Katrinka. She had no family. I wanted her to have something stable in her life. I encourage her to attend university because girl cannot be spy for all time."

"Wow!" Fay exclaimed. "It is a wonderful ending for Katrinka. Thank you, Sasha."

"As you Americans say," Sasha went on, "but wait, there is more."

Fay chuckled. "I love it when there is more!"

Sasha motioned for Fay to lean toward him. "Faya, come near." He lowered his voice to a whisper. "After one year in GU service," he said, "routine medical testing had been conducted. The testing revealed Katrinka's ancestry linked her to Grand Duchess Natalya Veriskaya."

"I don't know this person. Who is she?" Fay asked.

"The Grand Duchess is the headship of the Imperial Family of Russia," Sasha explained. "A descendent of the Romanovs, the last Tsar of Russia."

"Jezus H! Sasha!" Fay cried. "You did blow up my brain! Is Katrinka aware of her ancestry?"

"No, it has been kept from her. Mostly to protect her safety. And what do you do with such a girl? Tell her she is in line for head of the Imperial Family of Russia?" Sasha shrugged his shoulders. "What can she do?" he went on. "What if she does not care? Her life now is arguably a normal one. You see her now, Faya. Her heart sings. You have made big impression on her. She now wants to be like you. And what if this information causes her heart to break?"

"I feel so honored, Sasha, but I agree." With

concern, Fay asked, "Will you one day tell her?"

"I will when I think she is ready for it," Sasha replied. "I believe now is not a good time. In meantime, she has protection of the state and may well be a state treasure. Depends on political climate of the time." Sadness crossed Sasha's face. "The last Tsar of Russia and his family were executed for political reasons," he said. "But to tell girl who dreams of the dance or serving a fellow man as nurse would vanish if she learned she might be next Grand Duchy of Russia. I, too, worry one day the present Grand Duchess will die. There would be millions of rubles for heir to inherit."

"As glamorous as it sounds, I can somewhat relate," Fay remarked. "I disliked being the daughter of America's elected king. I would rather have traded places with any girl in America. I understand your conflicts."

"Perhaps when the day arrives for me, you will help me with decision?" Sasha requested.

Fay promised, "Without question, my friend."

Sasha said, "I will have Katrinka meet you here tomorrow. I will tell her about your travel from future. It will make it easy for you."

"Because I will recall none of this when I return to the future," Fay said, "I will return to ask for your help again."

Fay had wondered about Kat since the first time she had met her. As Fay pieced together her first trip to Moscow, it dawned on her while she had been in the city, someone had had her six for the entire time. It made sense. Jon could not watch her twenty-four seven. He had to rest. During the times she had not been sleeping, she had been with either Sasha or Kat. Other times, it had been Jon, and probably Irishka, lurking unseen in the shadows. This time, E-Team had her six. She was never alone.

****

7:30 P.M., Rossiya Hotel, Moscow, Russia

Fay returned to her room feeling more confident about her operation than she had when the day had begun. And what Sasha had revealed to her about Katrinka, she could not even begin to fathom. The topic of Katrinka offered a lot for her to digest.

Fay had not seen hide nor hair of E-Team since the morning meeting. She knocked on the inner-connecting room door between James's room and her room. James answered.

"Come in!" James said. He and Kimo had their weapons apart on a table.

Typical commando stuff, Fay thought. These guys seemed to always be cleaning something weapons related.

James pointed to one of the comfortable chairs in the room. "Have a seat," he offered.

Fay sat. This was the first time during the day when she could unwind.

"How did your day go?" Kimo asked.

"I feel like I accomplished something," Fay replied. "Lavrov agreed to help me. With his help, I can get farther quicker than I would without his help. He will open doors for me. Lavrov has people to help. Hackers, safecrackers, and a femme fatale to keep Justine busy if I need to search his hotel rooms for what it is we are here for." Fay worried about Katrinka. "I am worried about the agent who will be occupying Justine. Can we spare someone to watch her six?" she requested.

James said, "I don't know of a Russian agent, male or female, who cannot more than handle an op. Rest easy; one of us will have her back."

"Thank you, guys," Fay replied. "This means a lot to me."

Fay wished Kimo and James goodnight and returned to her room. James and Sasha were right. Kat could take care of herself. But would Justine prove to be too much for young Kat to manage? Fay knew her mind would not let her sleep. Two bottles of rum from the minibar and she was out like a light, as they said, thirty minutes later.

****

Fay awoke at 7:35 A.M. She needed coffee, food, to meet with E-Team for the daily game plan, and to meet with Kat. She would also need to explain who Faye King was and the concept of time travel, without revealing top-secret information. It would be a delicate meeting.

Fay prepared herself for the day. She knocked on the door separating her room from James and Kimo's room. She chatted with them briefly. She told them she would meet with Katrinka at the Zhivago at 10:30 hours. She would leave her room at 10:00 hours. Following her meeting, she would return to the hotel to meet with the team to plan her next steps. Then, Fay returned to her room and ordered room service coffee and breakfast.

At 10:00 hours, Fay left her room dressed in a dark business suit. Andrew and Matthew escorted her from the hotel. Once they were on the street, the two men blended into the morning pedestrian sidewalk traffic. She was safe knowing the guys had her six.

Fay arrived at the Grand Café Doctor Zhivago at 10:15 hours. She wanted to ensure she was the first to arrive.

Katrinka arrived on time. When she entered, she began searching for Fay. Fay stood and waved to gain Kat's attention. Kat approached Fay with a wary and unsure look in her eyes.

"Kat," Fay said. "Sasha asked you to meet me."

Katarina appeared confused. Then a smile came to her lips. "How?!" she exclaimed.

"Katrinka, please sit with me," Fay requested.

Kat sat with hesitation. She spoke. "How is this? Sasha tell me you travel in time and we will meet again in future." She studied Fay.

"My dear Katrinka," Fay said, "I will explain." With a reassuring smile, Fay asked, "Shall we order something?"

"Please. I have now just come from university. It is time I eat," Kat replied.

The waitperson approached their table.

Fay asked Kat, "What will you order?"

Kat spoke to the waiter in Russian. He smiled and asked, in Russian, what would be her order.

Fay replied in English, "I will have the same."

The waiter left. Fay asked, "What did we order?"

Kat giggled. "One thing I already like about you, Fay, is you trust me."

"Thank you. It is a generous compliment."

"Is true. We order croissants with ham and coffee. Is okay?" Kat wanted to know.

"Perfect," Fay replied. "I know you have questions. I will tell you in due time."

"Sasha say you are friend. He does not lie to me," Kat replied. "How can I help you?"

"I am on a Navy mission where I must wear a disguise," Fay told the other woman. "When we meet again in the future, I will appear not as the same person to you.

Katrinka nodded her head. "Sometimes things must be done another way," she acknowledged. "Disguise is so good. This is very good undercover."

"For what I am doing, no one must know it is me. I am someone else," Fay told her.

Katrinka again offered a knowing nod.

"My dear, what do you study at university?" Fay inquired.

"I study engineering." Kat smiled. "But I think I am not interested in driving train all my life."

Fay was not ready for Kat's quick humor. She laughed. "That's a good one. I will have to remember it. Although I have been told I will not recall any of this meeting. All you tell me now, you must tell me again," she remarked.

Katrinka gave Fay an unsure nod. "Truth is, it is boring," Kat divulged. "Sasha advises me. I appreciate his concern, but it is not me."

"What would you do instead?" Fay asked her.

"I like dance, but no good jobs in dance. I like nurse, but too many nurse already," Kat answered. "So, I do not know."

"Career choices are hard," Fay said with sympathy. "I understand your conflict."

Their breakfast order arrived. "*Spacibo*," Fay said to the waiter.

Kat sipped at her coffee. She buttered her croissant, then took a bite and asked, "Will you learn Russian one day?"

"I do not think so. Now, I speak Italian and French fluently. English, not so good," Fay quipped.

Kat laughed. "You joke with me. One day I hope to be fluent with the English. And someday, I will teach you Russian." Katrinka asked, "We did not talk about this in future?"

"We only met for a short time," Fay told her. "My mind was elsewhere. You will ask me questions about your English language study."

"Yes, I want perfect English," Kat asserted.

Fay reassured her, "You speak English well."

"You help me in future when we meet?" Kat guessed.

"I was honored to help you, Kat." Fay, again, smiled. "I asked you to meet me because I would like your help."

"Of course. What is it I am doing?" Kat asked.

"I am here to obtain information from a bad man," Fay explained. "I have an idea how you can help me get it."

"I am good at getting information," Kat said. "Sometimes it is my work."

"This man has secret documents I must have for my government before the Chinese government gets it," Fay told her. "It is very urgent for me."

"You want me to keep this man busy while you get this information?" Kat speculated.

"Are you interested, Kat?"

"Too much, I think."

"I must warn you this man is perilous for women," Fay stated. "He is known to harm or even kill them. He is what we in America call a 'sex predator.'"

"I know these men," Kat replied. "When I was thirteen years old, I have to work to support my old mother and father. I learned men with influence prefer cute little girls like me. I can get big money from them if I need it."

"How old are you, Kat?" Fay inquired.

"Now twenty-three years," Kat responded. "For me, I am only good to government employer for maybe five years. Then I am too old. I must have something else."

Fay guessed, "You are military then?"

"Yes, I have special military job. Sasha knows I need better, so he explains me I must go to university," Kat answered. "University is free for all Russians. He said engineering is good. He is right, of course. I don't like it."

"Would you consider ever living in the United States?" Fay wondered.

"Yes, my friend Mishka went to United States. She met cute boy. Is now working in bank and is happy. For me, I have no opportunity. I have more money than I will ever need. Men are generous when drunk. They are stupid. They give me everything. I have no hope of visa without sponsor." Kat shrugged her shoulders. "For me," she said, "it is dream."

"I agree. Some men can be stupid," Fay replied. "But there are good men too. Sasha is a good man."

"He is. But rare, I think. You know, Faya," Kat went on, "many Russian men drink and smoke. Average life, I am told, for Russian man is sixty years. Russian woman is ninety years. What do I do? Marry guy, he dies, and for next thirty years then what do I do?"

"You would work at a good job and have lots of grandchildren," Fay responded.

"Correct! For now, a babushka I am not. Someday may be okay, but I have to get to someday first," Kat insisted.

Fay listened with great sympathy. She offered a comforting smile. "Thank you for sharing," she told Kat. "Let's get through these next few days. I may have a few ideas for you."

"Is good." Kat's eyes were bright with joy. "What am I to do with the creepy man?" she asked.

Fay instructed, "I want you to find out where his business office is. You may have to follow him to learn it."

"I am good at following, Faya," Kat promised. "Is all I have to do?"

"For now. Once I know where his office is, I have something else for you. Okay?"

Kat agreed. Fay wrote down Justine's name and hotel address for Kat.

"I will warn you," Fay told Kat. "Do not - do not ever allow yourself to be alone with this man. He is evil with women. I am serious when I say he may injure you." Fay reached across the table and grasped Kat's hand. "Will you promise me?"

Kat placed her free hand over the top of Fay's hand. "I promise, Faya."

"Okay! If you find his office, text me," Fay requested.

Kat agreed, and the two women parted. Fay was apprehensive for Kat's safety, yet Kat had developed, during her short life, instincts and intuitions concerning male behaviors that had given her an understanding most women did not develop in a lifetime. Russian agents were, by nature, not weak.

Fay returned to her room at the Ritz Carlton. Exhausted, she quickly fell asleep.

****

The chiming of her cell phone woke Fay. She had received a message from Kat: *I found office! Should we meet?*

The kid was fast! Fay texted Kat back: *Same time, same place. Today?*

Shortly, Kat returned the text: *Da!*

Fay then met with James. She would order a room service breakfast, remain at the hotel until 10:00 hours, then travel to the Zhivago for her 10:30 meeting with Katrinka. After the meeting, she would return to meet with E-Team to plan their next move.

Once at the café, Fay chose the same table they had sat at the day prior. Kat arrived at 10:30 A.M. She smiled and waved when she noticed Fay.

She sat. "Hi, Faya!" Kat seemed excited. "I found office," she said.

"Outstanding!" Fay exclaimed. "It did not take you long."

"I went to hotel. Wait in lobby," Kat recounted. "Justine came to lobby. I follow him to room. I know room. I went back to desk. I learn it was suite. Boy at desk said many men come and go all day to this room. What can it be?"

"An office. Nice job!" Fay smiled. "Let's get something for you. Have you eaten?" she asked.

"No. I can eat coffee, croissant, and ham. Is good!" Kat paused. "Maybe bottle of wodka." She read the shocked look on Fay's face. "Just joke," she assured the other woman. "Sasha said you are afraid of wodka." She laughed.

Seeing Katrinka laugh, when considering her tragic life, warmed Fay to know life remained in Katrinka's heart. Kat had the heart of a survivor.

"Faya, what do we do now?" Kat wanted to know.

"Can I text you later today?" Fay asked. "We'll meet again. You do not have school today?"

"Maybe Sunday school." Kat giggled. "Today is Sunday. No school."

"Sunday?" Fay realized she had completely lost track of the week.

Afterwards, Fay met with James and the team. They decided Katrinka would begin her task of distracting Justine, allowing Fay sufficient time to search Justine's office for the documents.

Fay asked, "Did you guys know it was Sunday?" Other than looks of doubt evident on a few of their faces, all nodded yes.

Fay next contacted Sasha. She asked for a meeting at his earliest convenience. Sasha asked if she could meet him at Kremlin. Sasha told her to go to the first gate on the right side of Lenin. He would allow her access to Kremlin. She should be there at 19:00 hours that evening.

Fay arrived at the gate at five minutes to seven. Sasha was waiting for her. One of the two soldiers opened the gate and stood aside as Fay passed through.

"Good evening, Faya," Sasha said. "Welcome to Kremlin."

Fay smiled. "*Spacibo*, Sasha," she replied.

"We make short walk to Twelve Apostle's Church," Sasha told her.

Five minutes later, Fay and Sasha entered the small church. A woman wearing a scarf stood near the entrance. The scarf hid the woman's face.

Sasha nodded in the person's direction. "We will sit." He pointed to a bench in the last row of the cathedral. The woman moved and sat in the next row forward.

The woman turned. She removed her scarf. Fay recognized her.

"Irishka," Fay said, "good to see you."

"They did good job," Irishka said. "I did not know you."

Fay had met Irishka when she had attended the Governor's Ball in Seattle. Irishka would know how Fay truly appeared without her current disguise. Irishka had been all business then, and Fay sensed Irishka had long past dispensed with pleasantries. Not a "hello, how are ya" sort of gal.

Fay nodded and smiled. Fay recalled President Rudkovsky had told Irishka her help would be needed. It appeared Irishka's help would be needed again.

"Faya, you will need Irishka's help for search of Justine's office," Sasha said. "It is too dangerous to do this alone."

Sasha's proposal had merit. Irishka was Russian Navy special forces. Fay would be well protected.

"You will text me when you are ready to move. Yes?" Irishka asked. "I will meet you where you say."

"It is simple. As soon as Katrinka has Justine occupied, we will search the office." Fay asked Sasha, "What about a safe?"

"Irishka will have man who can break safe and has camera if you need photos," Sasha replied. "He is trusted, so no worry."

The meeting was simple and quick. Irishka departed the church. Sasha and Fay sat for a few minutes, and they too then left the church. Sasha walked with Fay to her hotel. She was aware two E-Team members had eyes on her as well. She truly believed she had more protection now than when she had been a First Daughter. Fay and Sasha said goodnight. Fay went to her room at 21:30 hours. Time for two tiny bottles of rum from the minibar.

While Fay waited to drift off to sleep, she thought about Katrinka and Irishka. It occurred to her both women were, coincidentally, of the same stature, as well as the same height, weight, and hair coloring. Fay had assumed all along Irishka was to be the one who would assassinate Evilenko. Inspector Popov had admitted to Fay she fit the description given of the one who had killed Evilenko in the Arbat bar. Now she was left to wonder, might it be Katrinka? Based on her limited information, Fay knew Irishka to be a Russian Navy commando, a counterpart to Jon Shaman. Sasha had told her, and Katrinka had admitted to employment by the Russian government, yet she did not seem the commando type - more the Sparrow type. Both women would be capable assassins.

Chapter 19

Fay met with the entire team in James's suite. Today, Katrinka would distract Justine long enough for Irishka, Irishka's tech guy, and Fay to search Justine's office for the schematics. Andrew seemed smitten by Kat. He mentioned her many times. Fay would not deny his assessment of the woman. Justine would notice the stunning girl in a heartbeat.

Fay explained to the team Katrinka planned to hang out in the lobby of Justine's hotel. By habit, Justine dined around 19:00 hours. Katrinka hoped to finesse a dinner invitation. Suppose she could stretch it out for approximately ninety minutes. In that case, it should give her team enough time to disable the office surveillance and to hack computers and crack a safe. The Russians were reputed to have the best hackers in the world. Fay was unaware of how adept the Russian safecracker was.

Fay told the team, Irishka, and her tech guy, to meet at the Zhivago at 18:30 and wait for Kat's signal. She made a mental note to find out the tech guy's name. One team, which probably included Andrew, would monitor Katrinka and Justine. Katrinka would work without a headset or other communication. By nature, Justine would be ever vigilant. If he got a hint of impropriety, the op would be blown. The kid would be on her own, although Andrew and Matthew planned to work a hand

204

signal system with her. Andrew would relay information from Katrinka to the entire team.

James had mentioned vaguely E-Team had run an op with Irishka before. He had confidence in her focus. He and two team members would back up "Team Mary." Fay texted Kat and Irishka to reconfirm the op was a go. Fay would hang out in her room until it was time to meet with Irishka at the Zhivago.

****

18:10 Hours, Ritz Carlton, Moscow Russia

Fay left her hotel room at the preplanned time. Kimo was waiting near the elevator. He would escort her to the Zhivago, where she planned to arrive ahead of Irishka and her tech guy. Fay and Kimo arrived a few minutes ahead of schedule.

Irishka smiled. Fay had noticed she did not smile often. "Sorry we are late," Irishka said. She offered her hand in the direction of the man standing beside her. "Oleg," she said. "Oleg, is Faya."

Fay gathered Oleg to be light on English, but he did smile with a slight nod of his head and said, *"Dobriy vecher."*

Fay knew the greeting to mean, "Good evening." Fay returned, *"Spasibo, vam togo zhe." ("Thank you, same to you.")*

The three found a nearby table and sat.

"Oleg is brother," Irishka said. "Best geek all Russia." She seemed very proud.

Fay recalled Sasha had told her Katrinka was his daughter. This left Fay wondering about the brother's validity.

Oleg spoke to Irishka in Russian. Irishka listened to him patiently. She turned to Fay. "Oleg say he has security system figured already," Irishka translated. "He said is easy for him."

What a gem Oleg had turned out to be. His proactive approach to analyzing the office system would save them a lot of time. He would have more time to focus on the safe and the computer. Fay reminded them while in the office, if they moved something, they must ensure they replaced it in precisely the same spot they had removed it from. They needed to be mindful of losing personal items. Irishka assured her they had nothing which could inadvertently be left behind. They would wear booties on their shoes. Now, they waited for Katrinka to report she had Justine's complete and undivided attention.

Fay confided in Irishka her worry about Katrinka and Justine.

"No worry. I have worked with her before," Irishka consoled Fay. "Is maybe ten years with these men. She is best."

Irishka's vote of confidence felt reassuring. Fay knew Kat's very different side. She could not help having a motherly concern.

They waited. Then, Irishka, who was now in contact with Andrew, said, "Katrinka has success. We go."

One dangerous event was enough for any woman. Fay had stopped counting at three in the last three years! A nondescript car waited at the door. The walk would have been a short one, yet time was critical. Katrinka would have scant minutes to keep Justine occupied.

The car stopped at the rear entrance of the hotel. Kimo stood near the rear door. Fay noticed when Irishka passed near Kimo, Kimo mentioned something to her. Irishka smiled but did not speak to him. *How would they know one another?* Fay wondered.

Oleg carried a tool bag. He resembled a hotel building engineer.

A service elevator shot Fay and the crew to the hotel's sixth floor. The hall seemed deserted. Yet, she knew one or more E-Team commandos were nearby. When they arrived at Justine's apartment office door, Oleg went to work on a small electrical security panel at the right side of the door.

Oleg said something to Irishka. "Oleg says system is the crap," Irishka translated for Fay.

Good news. One minute later, the three entered Justine's room. Oleg began searching the walls for a safe. It would be faster to search the safe first in the event the documents were there. Fay assumed they were looking for a thumb drive. She and Irishka searched everything, from the drawers to the bookshelf.

Irishka stopped. She pressed her finger to her left ear. "Andrew says Justine is returning to room," she informed them. "Katrinka says he forgot something. We must leave."

The three moved to the door. Once outside the room, Oleg reset the security system. A door opened across the hall from Justine's room. Irishka took Fay's arm and pushed her into the room. These spies had thought of everything.

They were not a second too soon. Irishka watched while Justine disarmed the security system then swiped the door card, allowing him to enter the room. Katrinka had not left the table, indicating Justine planned to return. A hand signal from Katrinka to Andrew assured them all was well.

Team Mary waited. When Justine emerged from the room five or so minutes later, they remained in place.

When Andrew confirmed to Irishka that Justine had been reseated with Katrinka, Irishka confirmed the time to move.

Once again, Oleg disarmed the security system. Fay admired his skill. Shortly after, they were back in the room searching for the schematic - if the documents were even there. Oleg had found the safe. There were only so many walls. Yet, it was a problematic task nonetheless. He reported the safe was not as simple as the security system. He began working, while Fay and Irishka continued looking everywhere for anything that would resemble the plans.

After ten minutes of searching and safe cracking, Oleg spoke to Irishka. "Oleg wants you to come to safe," Irishka told Fay.

The secure door opened, and Oleg stood grinning like the Cheshire Cat. He motioned for Fay to review the contents of the safe. There were thumb drives and one set of what appeared to be paper plans. She scooped all of it into her backpack. Oleg shut the safe, and the three exited the room. Oleg reset the security system.

Fay did not know if they had found what they were looking for. Again, the three transited to the hotel rear entrance and the waiting car. Fay knew they had not gone undetected, but Kat remained with Justine. A call to the lady's room would clear her from her dinner with Justine during the evening. Fay worried when Justine realized he had been robbed, he would suspect Katrinka. He would search Moscow for her. Yet, Fay had met Kat at the airport in the future after Fay and Jon had shot Justine. She knew he did not find Kat. The future was set. Kat would be safe from Justine.

The car did not stop but went directly to Kubinka

Airbase, where E-Team waited. There were smiles and congratulations. As the chopper engines wound up, James, Andrew, Kimo, and Matthew had a brief, animated discussion with Irishka. The laughter and back-patting confirmed in Fay's mind Irishka and E-Team had served together in the past. Before boarding the chopper, Fay handed an envelope to Irishka. She asked her to please see Katrinka got it. Irishka assured Fay Katrinka would receive it without fail. Fay and the team boarded the chopper. Oleg and Irishka reentered the car. Fay waved as she watched the car speed off into the night.

Silence prevailed during the long flight aboard the Russian chopper as it made its way back to *Deception Pass* and the future. The helicopter touched down on the helo pad on *Deception Pass*. The team disembarked, and once safe from the turning blades, the chopper lifted off and flew east into the pre-dawn sun.

The team went directly to the departure/arrival room. They stowed their gear. The tech geeks helped them strap in. A shot in the arm, and the countdown began. *Ten-nine-eight...zero.* Fay experienced a mild headache. Otherwise, in her mind, one second had passed since she had last noted the time on the departure countdown clock. The only indication anything had occurred was that she was wearing different clothing than she had been the second before.

Fay said to Kimo, sitting next to her, "We traveled in time, and they were right. I do not recall any of it. I suppose we will soon learn if we succeeded or not."

Deception Pass came to rest three hundred miles from Saint Petersburg harbor. They would rest and recuperate. A chopper will pick them up, transporting them to Porkkala Naval Base in Finland. From there, they would fly commercial air to Helsinki, then to London Heathrow, and next to Seattle-Tacoma International Airport. Fay's memory had recorded a meeting with Admiral May and James, as well as mention of a teleport aboard *Deception Pass*. An op, and then back. That is what she recalled: a trip to *Deception Pass* and back. What fun.

On arrival at Bremerton and several days later, Admiral May called Fay and her E-Team for a meeting. He and several other high-ranking officers accompanied him. All were beaming with joy. The team was congratulated on a successful mission, one none of them remembered. It felt good to know they had done something worthwhile. Maybe someday, someone would share it with them.

****

Several days later, Fay was chatting with JP and Winslow. "Hey, I got like nine Seahawks tickets," she told them. "Sunday, season opener. Fifty-yard line. Does anyone want to go?"

JP and Winslow could not say yes fast enough.

Fay's cell chimed. It was a confusing text from Kat: *I am airport. Can you meet me?*

What airport? Fay messaged back. *I don't understand, Sweetie. Which airport?* Fay had thought herself to be beyond any shocking event she had experienced lately.

Seattle, Kat replied via text.

If a person's heart could sing and stop at the same time, Fay's did that day. Fay called Kat's cell number.

Kat answered, "*Da*. Faya, it's me. Kat!"

"I am so happy!" Fay replied. "You should come to me. Take a taxi. Tell the driver you want to go to

Bremerton Navy Base. You got that?"

"Bremerton Navy," Kat repeated, "yes."

"The travel will be about one hour. Don't worry. On your way, let me know the taxi company's name, and I will have Shore Patrolman meet your car at the main gate," Fay instructed. "One of the people at the gate will bring you to me."

"Got it."

Fay had not yet told JP or Winslow about the first trip she had taken to Moscow - the one she remembered. What do you say? *I went to Moscow and killed a man?* But she did want them to know Katrinka and what made her special. Fay did not yet understand Kat's miraculous arrival in the United States.

Fay watched from the window. A taxi pulled up. Kat got out of the car. Her radiance brightened the day. The kid traveled well! She paid the fare. The driver retrieved her luggage from the car's trunk. An SP vehicle had led them in. The sailor grabbed her luggage and walked her to the entrance to JAG Corps. Fay beat them to the door. Both women hugged. There were many tears, and there may have been a little shrieking as well. Fay wanted Kat to meet Winslow and JP. The women continued on to Fay's office.

"Why are you here?!" Fay asked. "I can't believe you are here!"

Kat handed Fay an envelope. Fay accepted it.

"Open it," Kat said.

The envelope had Katrinka's name on it; Fay recognized the handwriting as her own. But she had never written a letter to Kat, had she?

Fay read the letter aloud: "Dear Me, you have written this and given it to Irishka to give to Katrinka. I am on a mission in Moscow, one I know I will not remember. I told Katrinka she should consider moving to the USA when she is ready to leave her life in Moscow. Have her tell me about our conversation. Love, Me."

The letter had been written in Fay's handwriting and scented with her perfume.

After her long flight, Kat was tired and hungry. Fay declared a half-day off for her crew. She invited JP and Winslow to have lunch with her and Kat. After, they were welcome to come to her condo to better get to know Katrinka. All agreed.

Following lunch and knowing Kat needed rest, Fay was too curious to know about a past she did not recall. The four arrived at Fay's condo. Kat proved eager to talk about it from her point of view. While JP and Winslow settled in, Fay took Kat to her kitchen, intending to prepare coffee and tea. As she prepared the beverages, Kat spotted the small aquarium.

She tapped on the glass. "What is it in vat, Faya?" Kat asked.

"They are my pets, Joey and Garfield," Fay explained. "The little colorful one is a guppy."

"A what-pea?" Kay repeated, confused.

"A guppy." Fay spelled it for her.

"Huh. Faya, this goopea is not enough," Kat said. "It is for eating? Yes?"

Kat was serious. Fay tried not to laugh. "Did you have a pet in Russia?" she asked the other woman.

"Never. All my life, I always wanted cat. Small. My life did not allow it," Kat replied. "What you call it?"

"A kitten?" Fay guessed.

"Yes, I think baby cat."

Fay had recently pawned her pest cat, Barnacle Bill, off on Captain Towsley. "My dear," Fay said, "you will live here until you are ready to go on your own. And we will get the kitten for you. Okay?"

"Is best I can hope for. Thank you, Faya!" Kat whispered. "I brought money. Maybe it will help you?"

Not wanting to be nosy, Fay said, "We can open a bank account for you. The Military Federal Credit Union is near. We will go there tomorrow."

"Will bank accept two hundred thousand U.S.?" Kat asked.

"You have a lot of money, sweetie," Fay observed.

"I saved money since thirteen years old," Kat explained. "I dreamed one day of coming to America. I would give it to man who said he would help me go to America, but I think he was mafia. I no do it. Your letter made me think about it. I showed to Sasha. He went to government and got visa. He say I go to you. You will help me." Kat frowned. "Is okay?"

"It is beyond okay," Fay reassured her. "Today, we will call Sasha and tell him you are here with me and safe."

"Yes, is good plan. So, kitten and nice boy. Nice and cute boy, I think?" Kat asked.

"My sister and I are both experts in the cute, nice boy department," Fay told her. "Consider it done!"

Today, Fay had adopted a daughter. She had secretly harbored the idea of one day having a daughter. Her situation had never allowed for it. Katrinka was perfect for the role. Fay would have it no other way.

Fay and Kat returned to the living room with coffee, tea, and good news. All were anxious to hear Kat's life story. When she had finished, amazement and sadness touched the group. Fay did not know she had already learned about Kat's past when she had traveled back in time. After hearing about Kat's tragic life, her heart broke again. She now knew why she had written the letter to Kat in the past. Fay vowed Kat's life going forward would never know such heartache again. There was so much joy and goodness in Kat's heart waiting to be unbound. Katrinka deserved much better. Fay swore whatever it took, she would work to set the Sparrow free.

****

Mid-September, Luman Field, Seattle, Washington

Commander Faydra Green, Captain and Mrs. Egan Fletcher, Petty Officer First Class Don Winslow, Katrinka Lavrova, and Navy Captain Vern Towsley had hotdogs and beers in hand. They were all wearing shirts with the name "Markham" printed on the back, along with his player number, fifteen. They were prepared for the big game. Good luck blessed the day. Petty Officer First Class Andrew Lawrence was on leave, following the forgotten op in Moscow.

It had taken zero arm twisting by Fay to convince Andrew to join Fay and her group for the big game. In Andrew's mind, he had not yet met Katrinka. Fay now knew the story of her trip to the past from Kat's viewpoint. The story of the two dolphins and Andrew, who had saved Fay from drowning during an op in Korea, fascinated Kat. Andrew would be the perfect introduction to make to Katrinka.

The fifty-yard line seats, courtesy of player fifteen, gave them an excellent view. They all waited with great anticipation for the kickoff for the football game between the hometown pro football team versus their natural rival, the San Francisco pro football team. Former NCIS agent Corry Markham was suited up for his first game as a backup running back to superstar Chris Bennett.

"I am so happy and proud for Corry," Fay said to the group. "I hope he gets a chance to play today."

"He will, ma'am," JP predicted. "Bennett is old. He's going to get tired somewhere during the game."

A loud roar filled the stadium when the Seattle team took the field. Fay and her party rose in unison with the screaming fans, with yells and whistles to greet the team.

"GO, CORRY!" Fay yelled.

The time for the kickoff had arrived. To almost everyone's surprise, Coach Brandt decided to have Corry return the opening kickoff. The away team's kicker sent the ball into the end zone. Corry snatched the pigskin; be it nerves, perhaps, he dropped the ball. He hesitated to consider whether it was better to down the ball in the end zone. Instead, he snatched the ball from the ground and took off with blinding speed heading up field. In the end, only the last San Franciscan, the kicker, managed to trip him up. Corry landed on his back at the away team's forty-six-yard line. He had managed to run fifty-nine yards, giving the home team an excellent field position for their opening drive.

The seventy-two thousand Seattle fans went wild, chanting, "Corry, Corry, Corry!" Then, the crowd held their collective breaths as Corry lay motionless on the field. The concerned coach and trainers rushed to the aid of their fallen player. The team trainers talked to Corry, then the cheering returned when Corry hopped to his feet. As he jogged from the field under his own power, he, knowing where Fay and her crew were seated, pointed in Fay's direction with a giant smile on his face. The excited star running back Chris Bennett was the first player to greet his heir apparent as he neared the sidelines.

An exciting game came to an end, with the home team losing in a squeaker by three points on a last-second San Francisco field goal. Corry had endeared himself to Seattle fans worldwide.

Fay and her group made their way to the exit. Someone brushed by Fay. She stopped and turned to excuse herself. She spotted a tall, dark man disappearing into the crowd. Fay grabbed JP by her arm in an attempt to gain her attention. When she had it, she pointed towards the man.

JP confirmed, "Carson."

A word about the author...

Except for time spent in military service I live in the Pacific Northwest with my legal-beagle son K-K. and seven large tropical fish from the Amazon River. I am a second-generation Seattleite (that's what they call those of us who dwell in the shadow of Mr. Rainier). I have had the opportunity to travel our planet many times over. My stories are created from my memories of my personal experiences, the places I have visited, and the people and friends I have known.